MOMMA'S LITTLE HARRY

BOOKS BY GORDON BUNKER

FICTION

IN AMERICA
MOMMA'S LITTLE HARRY

NONFICTION

THE MAKING OF A MOTORCYCLIST
SUMMERS IN A TENT

GORDON BUNKER

MOMMA'S LITTLE HARRY

Thanks to
Kenster

Gladys sets herself into the La-Z-Boy and peers intently at him. She's thinking, this boy come out to interview me an hes sittin in my trailer home nervous as a cat. Gladys is nervous too, but determined to not let it show. She squints through her trifocals at his card, thinking, damn I never know which one is which to look through. All Im tryin to do is read his card. Clifford... Whats his last name? Gladys tips her head back. Bagsley. Clifford Bagsley, I bet hes outta Colorada. Lotta Bagsleys outta Colorada. Hes a reporter—first one ever want to speak with me, brave enough, or fool enough—with *The Panhandle Trumpet.*

Most folks don't even know Oklahoma's got a panhandle. Comes as no surprise. There isn't a whole hell of a lot going on out here, which for most is just fine. Of course folks here still know how to enjoy themselves a little bit. "What is it youd like to know, young man?" Gladys asks.

"Well, Ms. Calloway, with the—"

"Gladys. Everbody calls me Gladys."

"Yes ma'am. I mean Gladys. With the controversial closing of your... establishment, we'd like to get your perspective. And—"

"We didnt do nothin wrong. Thats my perspective. You got that?" Gladys pauses and eyes Clifford, who nods innocently. "Make sure you say that. We didnt do nothin wrong. What I started here was a little nightclub. I recognized what my patrons wanted an what they come back for an I give it to em. Now if theres some sufferin from prudishness around here, well, I spose thats their problem, aint it? Not mine, you understand? There aint nothin on the books in Spriggs County that says havin a topless bar is against the law."

Clifford swallows. "Yes, ma'am."

Gladys figures she better let the young man get his notes down so she shuts up. The boy is scribbling into his little notebook on his knee fast as he can. She wants him to get it right. "Gladys will do," she says. "Somes call me a Madam, which aint the case, but to you, boy, its Gladys."

"I apologize Ms. Gladys. I mean Gladys," says Clifford.

Poor kid, thinks Gladys. Hes got manners which is more than most. I otta take it easy on him. Im just a tad heated up over all this gettin closed down bull-ticky. Ill soften my tune, make some charm on him. What the hell, mightn even be a little fun, get him to blush, a sixty-five-year-old woman gettin a boy still wet behind the ears to blush is always fun. "Can I offer you a little somethin to drink, Clifford?" Gladys asks with a touch of sweetness.

He looks up at her, an imposing figure spread out like a heavy cake batter in her chair. A little dazed, he smiles. "Yes, ma'... Gladys," he says. "Thank you. An ice tea would be nice, thank you." Clifford goes back to his scribbling.

Gladys cranks the wooden lever on the side of the chair forward and hoists her old lump of a body up and grabs the floor lamp to steady herself. The shade titters back and forth. "Wouldnt you like a little somethin perk it up a bit?" she asks. She's looking right at him, grinning. And damn if he doesn't blush! HOO HAW! She thinks. He does want a little somethin!

"Oh, um…" Clifford's gaze is locked in by Gladys'. He has to think about this proposition for a moment, then says a little sheepishly, "Well, thank you Gladys, but—"

"Course you would," she interjects. "You just keep scribblin and Ill just keep talkin, and ol Momma here will fix you up real nice." She notices he doesn't say anything for a moment. Collectin himself I spose, thinks Gladys, I give em just a little bit of a coquettish look, not full on, got to keep em wonderin. She smiles. Clifford plays the game and smiles back. Satisfied she's still got the charm, she lets her old hips roll as she saunters into the kitchen. Her trailer is open concept.

"Well Gladys, to some, even the name 'Momma's Little Harry' is, shall I say, a bit controversial. How did you arrive at that name?"

Gladys is pulling back the flip top on a can of ice tea and there's the old pang. She thought everybody knew by now, but apparently that's not the case. The boy must be new in town. Gladys ponders on this a moment and selects two Collins glasses from the shelf and puts a few ice cubes from the insulated bucket into each. She reaches under the bar for the bottle of Canadian Mist and sets it by the glasses. "Lookin back, that was a mistake," she says, pouring generous dollops of whiskey into the glasses.

"How so?"

"That over there," she points to the hand tinted studio photograph hanging in the breakfast nook. Big Daddy made the pine frame for it from some leftover door trim, and stained it nice, just like walnut. "Thats a picture of my boy Harry when he was nine," she says. "He never saw ten." Clifford looks at the picture of a cute little smiling boy, with blonde bangs cut at an awkward angle. Gladys tops off the glasses with the ice tea and slides a swizzle stick in each. She knows the finishing touches. But walking back into the living room even after what, forty years, she still feels that old heartbreak. Losing her boy, the only child she'd have.

"I'm awful sorry," says Clifford. "A terrible loss."

"Thank you Clifford," she says. "Youre a fine young man to say that."

"Please, call me Cliff."

She nods and says, "Push them magazines outta the way, if you would." Clifford slides them back with great care because the stack is tall and slippery and it's about to let go all over the place. Gladys sets his drink on the table. "There you go, Cliff." Their eyes meet and she gives him a wink. "Teas got a little extra in it."

"Thank you, Gladys." Clifford stirs the drink with the swizzle stick, takes a sip, and snorts back into the glass. His face contorts into a five alarm fire. Gladys eyes him and giggles as she sets back into the La-Z-Boy.

"My!" gasps Clifford. "There's quite a lot of a 'little extra' in this here tea!"

"Clifford, let me be frank." Gladys takes a healthy mouthful of her tea, swishes it back and forth between her teeth, swallows, lets out a sigh of satisfaction, and says, "Hits the spot. If theres one thing I learned from my little Harry, it was to enjoy whats set before us, ever moment, as best we can. Aint none of us know which one will be our last. Its the truth, an Harry taught me that the hard way." Gladys stares into her glass. "Harder for him than me." Clifford scribbles in his notebook. "An its cause a what I learnt from my little boy," continues Gladys. "God bless his soul in heaven, I even started my place. All of us mopin around in this "Golden Gardens" sinkhole of a retirement community. If its all so goddamned golden, why are we all such a bunch a sourpusses wanderin around? I spose what, waitin to die?" Gladys takes another gulp from her drink. "So I asked myself, why not spice it up a bit? I got to a few a my old gal friends here an put it to em straight. 'Lets us start a geriatric topless joint, right here in the trailer park!'"

Clifford is intent on his notes. What a story! Gladys figures she better slow down. Clifford finally stops writing and looks up. "Take a little sip a your tea, Cliff," she says, smiling.

Clifford complies. "Phewee," he says, wiping his mouth with the back of his hand. He's feeling it, and suggests, "Please Gladys, go on."

"An we call it Mommas Little Harry in my boys remembrance," she says nodding her head proudly, and adds, "Let em think what all they want. I call it *marketing*." Gladys smiles, pleased by her cleverness and thinks to herself, let the boy rest an enjoy his drink. "Take another sip a your tea. Relax for a minute, go on now an have a sip," she says. "I aint goin nowhere. Got all the time in the world."

Clifford relaxes and sits back in his chair. "Once you get used to it, this tea is pretty darn good," he says, and he's feeling good too. He looks at his notes. "Gladys, I can tell this is going to be quite some story."

"Oh yeah, it will be," says Gladys, smugly. "An you only gettin the tip a the ol iceberg so far."

"So you had friends interested in going in on this with you?"

"Yes-sir-ee, I did. Now you got to understand, an no disrespect, but one way or another for us women, our men leave us. Stick-to-itiveness in a man is rare as hens teeth. Now with my girls, as I call em, theres Grandma Bugbee, Miss Bunny, an Puss N. Boots, an me a course, an we aint really girls, thats just a marketing term. Wes women, oh yeah, wes women through an through. Anyway, none of us had husbands so we didnt feel like we had any kind a sanctity to protect. An we all thought yeah, this could be a hell of a lotta fun. An we might just turn a dollar, bettern what Uncle Sam pries outta his ol sock and sends us ever month. Dont have to be much to beat that! So we pooled our resources an bought the doublewide on lot 8B, thats over in the corner, on a repo. Didnt take much to gut it an fix it up. Real nice like."

Gladys sips her tea as does Clifford. Clifford nods his head. "How long were you open before getting shut down?" he asks.

Gladys' smile turns to a firey stare. "Six year, four month an eighteen days. Not like I was countin or anythin."

"Well that's a good run. Congratulations."

"Thank you. An we'd still be runnin if it weren't for that, that... *prude*." Gladys thinks for a moment. "You know, if it looks like a horse, smells like a horse, an kicks like one... its a horse."

"Yes ma'am," says Clifford as he jots that one down.

Gladys smirks, thinking my that boy has manners. Its them polite ones... bet he might just be a *wildcat* tween the covers. And she finds *herself* blushing! Gladys, you ol fool, she thinks, ol enough to be his maw. Twice over!

"Would it be possible to take a tour of the establishment?" asks Clifford.

"Wed be breakin the law if we did. Sheriff Dalhart put a lock on the door." But her face lights up, and she gets a crazy look in her eyes. "He didnt put one on the kitchen vent, though," she says, rubbing her hands together and snickering in a sinister way. "Youre not averse to a little lawbreakin are you, Cliff? All we need is bring over the stepladder."

"Well Gladys," says Cliff and he takes a good swallow of his tea, "being on assignment for the paper and all..." and he grins and slowly wobbles his head side to side, "but a little lawbreaking, strictly in the name of getting the story, you understand, is not a problem." He tips his glass up, drains it, and coughs. "So long as we don't get caught."

Clifford stands up a little too quickly and finds his head is spinning. "Gladys," he asks, "how much whiskey did you put in my tea?"

6

Gladys looks at him sheepishly. "Oh... enough."

Clifford shakes his head. He's thinking, his first assignment for *The Trumpet* and here he is getting drunk with a woman he doesn't know who's old enough to be his grandmother. He just got his Associate Degree in Journalism from High Plains Community College and they didn't say anything about it being like this. He stuffs his notepad in his front pocket. Whatever all happens he just better not lose his notepad. Gladys wobbles over to the bar and grabs her keys. It's a big bunch on a ring with a pink rabbit's foot dangling from it.

She waves the foot under Clifford's nose. "My niece Lily gave me this for good luck. Shes a nice girl. You might just like to meet her."

Clifford, suddenly doe-eyed, nods his head to at least be polite, but keeps his mouth shut. He helps Gladys down the steps out of the trailer. "Well borry a stepladder from Big Daddy, right over here." She points to the trailer next door. "Hes my neighbor, with *benefits*."

Clifford looks around. The place is a little rough. The back end of a motorcycle sticks out the door of a corrugated metal shed. Weeds are growing up through piles of old parts and batteries and a separate pile of sun-faded fire extinguishers. Spent, he presumes. The trailer sits up on jack stands, with no skirt or anything around the perimeter. A rusted Jeep sits in the driveway. They follow a dirt path around the trailer. Gladys doesn't attempt the rickety set of stairs leading to the door, so she leans over them and pounds her fist on the bottom of it.

It takes a moment before a voice from inside bellows, "WHO IS IT?!"

"Its... your... neigh... bor...," sings Gladys.

"JUST A MINUTE!"

Gladys turns to Clifford. "Youll like Dig Baddy." She giggles and haphazardly pats Clifford on his arm.

The trailer shakes and creaks. The louvered crinkle glass in the door rattles. And then the door opens. "Sorry Honeybunch, I…" The towering, massive hulk of Big Daddy stands in the door in his plaid boxer shorts and white muscle shirt. Well, it used to be white. He's scratching the exposed slice of his ample and hair-covered belly that's protruding between his shorts and shirt. "… whos *this?*" He pushes the wisps of hair that have fallen over his face out of the way and points at Clifford.

"Why this is Clifford Bagsley, Big Daddy. Clifford, meet Big Daddy." Gladys gestures for the two of them to shake hands. Or something. "Hes from *The Trumpet!* Come to get my story!" Gladys beams.

"Nice to meet you," says Clifford as he extends his hand up.

"Sorry. I was takin my afternoon nap," says Big Daddy. Hanging onto the door jamb to steady himself, he bends over, extending his hand to Clifford. It's a callused ham hock that engulfs Clifford's, and they can hear Clifford's knuckles crack as Big Daddy applies his grip. Clifford winces. "Nice to meet you, Clifford," he says, slowly shaking the boy's hand and sizing him up. He peers at Gladys and raises a bushy eyebrow. "You two been drinkin?"

Clifford feels a hot wave of apprehension wash through him. Word of this gets back to the office and this could be his first *and last* assignment. He stands still as a stone.

"We had a little refreshment, yes we did," says Gladys, nodding her head. She then flutters her eyelashes in an exaggerated way at Big Daddy.

"Least you could a done is invite me over," he says and winks at Clifford.

8

"Well Honeybuns, I didnt want to interrupt your nap. We know how important that is," says Gladys. She turns to Clifford. "Needs his beauty rest, as you can see."

Big Daddy self-consciously tugs the hem of his muscle shirt down over his boxer shorts. "If Id known this was gonna be a formal event, I woulda dressed for it. Wont you come in?" Standing there filling the door, he gracefully waves his arm into the trailer.

"Thats mighty neighborly a you," says Gladys, "but were on a mission. Id like to give Cliff here a tour a my *closed* establishment an wed like to borry your stepladder."

"Now Gladys, you know thats nothin but trouble. Sheriff impounded the property. County seal and everthin." Big Daddy's face turns to a picture of worry.

"Well just be there a minute. Just for my boys story. Well sneak in through the kitchen vent, no one ceptin us needs to know."

Big Daddy scratches inside his shorts. "Let me get some drawers on, an Ill come over with you. If nothin else, Ill keep a lookout." He doesn't wait for an answer, turns and mutters to himself, "Lord knows, I cant fit through that vent."

"See how nice he is?" Gladys says to Clifford.

"So important to have good neighbors," concurs Clifford.

Big Daddy comes back wearing filthy bib overalls and Sorel snow pac boots with the laces untied. He lumbers onto the stoop and slams the door shut. Staring at his boots at nearly eye level, Clifford wonders about those poor feet inside them. He also wonders why the glass in that door hasn't by now shattered into a million pieces. Big Daddy gingerly comes down the steps. They rock side to side as the metal footings sink into the ground. He looks himself up and down. "Best I could do on such short notice." He gives Gladys a little peck on the cheek. "Honeybunch, I do look ok, dont I?"

"You look fine, just fine," replies Gladys. "Mmm-*Mm!*" She collects and preens herself. "Lets not forget the ladder."

Big Daddy grabs it from beside the shed. "Well take the Toronado," says Gladys.

"No, lets take my Jeep," says Big Daddy.

"No, Honeybuns. Well take my car," says Gladys a little more firmly.

"Ill drive then," says Big Daddy. The old Toronado in front of Gladys' trailer lists to one side. The gold metallic paint is peeling and the vinyl top is blistering up, but at least the car's not all smashed up. Pretty good shape, considering what it's been through.

Gladys hands Big Daddy the keys. He holds them out at arm's length with his pinky sticking out and sneers at the dangling rabbit's foot. "Dont knock it, Honey, we can use all the good luck we can get!" she quips. Big Daddy grins as he throws the ladder in the cavernous trunk. Clifford clambers into the backseat and Gladys plops herself into the front.

Gladys has the driver's seat set way up forward, to the point Big Daddy can't even get in the car. He fiddles with the switches on the seat and mutters, "What was it, a *elf* last drivin this thing?" Gladys turns her head the other way, ignoring him. The seat slowly grinds back. "Thatll do," he says, squeezing himself in behind the wheel after tilting it way up to clear his belly. "Kinda like drivin a bus," he says as he turns the wheel left and right.

"Now cmon, Honeybuns," says Gladys. "Can we all just get a movin? Mr. Bagsley here dont have all day." Big Daddy eyes Clifford in the rearview mirror. Clifford shrugs his shoulders. Big Daddy starts the car and backs into the cloud of oily blue smoke pouring up from the tailpipe. The car creaks as Big Daddy eases it over the bar ditch, and off they go, like the Three Musketeers, chugging down the dirt street.

Clifford sits back, wondering how did he ever get himself into this one. He studies the different trailer homes as they roll by. They're all looking pretty grim, with sun-faded pieces of plastic trim broken and flapping in the breeze, one yard a maze of whirlygigs, sunflowers spinning, ducks on the wing, and tiny men sawing wood. Colored bottles lined up in the weeds glint in the sun. Clifford thinks it's grim, but Big Daddy and Gladys in the front seat seem to think it's fine. That's what matters, he supposes.

"Thats the so-called clubhouse on the left," chirps Gladys. She points her finger under Big Daddy's nose. Clifford peers at a low pitched-roof cinder block building with small windows. Just bare grey cinder block. Looks like the trim once had paint on it, but a long time ago. An ancient couple negotiate the front door and squint into the sun. They're both pushing walkers. The woman's is glistening candy-apple red, the man's is dull aluminum. The small Stars and Stripes affixed to his flutters in the breeze. Big Daddy toots the horn and waves. The old couple startle, but their tired faces light up, and they smile and manage to wave back. "Thats George and Betty Carson," says Gladys. "George was a regular customer at Mommas an Betty thought it was fine. She said to me, 'Let the old geezer have some fun. Hes given so much.' George is veteran a three wars," Gladys explains.

They stop and Gladys and Betty exchange pleasantries while George stares blankly at the sky. Gladys introduces Clifford, proudly pointing out he's from *The Trumpet* and is doing a story on her.

After the chitchat, they're again on their way. Big Daddy pilots the Toronado with authority, using the heel of one hand pressed to the wheel to turn it. He tips his head back to Clifford and says, "This ol destroyer has class."

Half hearing his comment Gladys snaps at him, "*What?*"

"Im talking bout the car," says Big Daddy.

They take a left and a right, and there in the corner lot, backed up against a barbwire fence, is Momma's. It's a double-wide, painted grey with a curvy purple stripe. Clifford can make out the bent glass tubes of a weather-beaten neon sign with two bare chested women flanking the name, "Mommas Little Harry - Grownup Fun." Gladys says, "Them women on the sign blink so it looks like their ninnies are bouncin. I paid a lot extra for that." A long ramp covered in Astroturf slopes up along the front to the door. "That ramp is for disabled," she says, adding, "Were up to code on everthin."

Clifford sees a steel bar with a padlock on it across the door and a sign that says, "IMPOUNDED by order of Spriggs County Sheriff - DO NOT ENTER. VIOLATORS…" The rest fades into a big block of fine print. Two official looking signatures are scrawled across the bottom in black marker. He's not entirely at ease with going in, and says, "Gladys, I'm thinking it's maybe not—"

"Oh, dont you worry your little head bout nothin," she says. She looks at Big Daddy. "Honeybuns, you think its OK, doncha?"

Big Daddy steers the car into the dirt lot and stops. He puts the transmission in P and says, "I guess so." But he's non-committal. "Ill keep my eyes open."

They clamber out of the car and Big Daddy gets the stepladder from the trunk. Clifford can tell Gladys is a touch nervous. Her eyes dart around, and she casts glances over her shoulders. The place is deserted but they are in plain view. Windows in nearby trailers stare like blank eyes. Gladys looks at Clifford and snickers. "The sign says do not enter, but far as we know its only talkin bout the front door."

"Far as you know," says Clifford, unconvinced.

"Aw cmon, were havin a little bit a *adventure!*" she says and snickers again. They make their way around back through thickets of prickly weeds and old steel drums and broken plumbing fixtures. Clifford moves tentatively. "Too cold for rattlers," says Gladys, "not to worry."

Clifford swallows hard. "Rattlers?"

A big stainless vent hood hangs on the back wall, with thick grease stains drizzling down from it. A wasp nest hangs from the bottom lip. Gladys picks up a stick and whacks it off. Clifford ducks while his heart jumps to his throat. "Too cold for them too," says Gladys.

Big Daddy plants the ladder below the hood. He wobbles it back and forth and looks at Clifford. "Itll be ok," he says, "Ill hold it."

"Now heres the plan," says Gladys. She looks at the two men. "This hood just lifts off. Me an Cliff will go in an Ill show him round. Big Daddy, you keep a eye out. Just round this corner you got a clear view a the road. You give three knocks on the vent if the Sheriff comes. Got that?"

Big Daddy solemnly nods his head. "What if its someone else?" he asks, adding, "Like you-know-who."

"Two knocks," says Gladys. She turns to Clifford. "The two a usll need to get on the ladder at once. The hood just lifts off but its heavy. Well hand it to Big Daddy. Ill go in first. You can help me if I get stuck." Clifford glances at Big Daddy, who's grinning like a fool, then nods his head. "Oh, an just inside is the

Fryolator. We didnt have a chance to empty the tubs before we got shut down, so watch your step. It might be slippry."

Gladys and Clifford climb opposing sides of the stepladder. They try lifting the vent hood but it doesn't budge. "Just give a little extra oomph to it!" cries Gladys. "Just lift!" She's working the thing with all her might, as is Clifford. It's coated with grease and dust and soot and it stinks. "Slippryer than greased goose poop," squeals Gladys, laughing. Clearly she's enjoying this. Clifford is not so sure. The hood starts to lift, then it pops off its perch. Gingerly so as not to drop it, but struggling, they hand it down to Big Daddy, who grabs it and with no effort sets it in the weeds. Looking quite satisfied, he wipes his hands on his bibs.

Gladys climbs up to the very top of the ladder, where it has the yellow safety sticker on it pointing out it's "NOT A STEP!"

She wiggles herself into the vent and says under her breath, "Oh my, guess we coulda done better cleanin this damn thing." Now her butt is sticking out and she's trying to raise the first foot.

Big Daddy looks at Clifford and winks. "Still put together pretty nice for a ol girl," he says in a half whisper. "Wish I had my camera."

"What was that?" yells Gladys, sounding like she's calling from the depths of some great echo chamber.

"Nothin," says Big Daddy. "You need a hand, Honeybunch?"

"No!"

Clifford helps himself to studying Gladys' behind. He turns to Big Daddy, nods, and sucks his teeth. "You're right."

Gladys gets one foot, then the other into the vent and wriggles herself in. There's some clanking and knocking and swearing, and Big Daddy and Clifford get laughing and they can't stop.

"I can hear you two!" comes the voice from the echo chamber. "What the hells so funny?"

"Nothing, Gladys," calls Clifford, mid-giggle.

"Dont know how the hell we gonna get outta here but…" comes the voice. "Your turn, smarty pants!"

Clifford casts an uneasy glance at Big Daddy, who directs the way up the ladder like an usher would to a seat at a wedding. Big Daddy grins. "Your turn, Cliff. Ill keep a eye out."

"My daddy used to say, 'God hates a coward,'" says Clifford as he climbs the ladder and pokes his head into the vent. Even for him, it's going to be a tight fit. It's disgusting. And dark. He takes a deep breath and climbs in. He can see Gladys looking at him, waving and encouraging him on. He puts his hand on the edge of the Fryolator, and it slips and plunges into a vat of cold grease up to his elbow. This *was* a new shirt he'd just bought at JCPenney for the job. The fat makes wet sucking sounds as he pulls his arm from it.

Gladys stands there in hysterics, laughing her head off and stamping her foot on the floor. In between gasps she says, "I told you, be careful!" Clifford scowls at her. He's not so happy. "Aw, Im sorry bout your shirt, Cliff," she says with a giggle, "but the look on your face!" With this she goes off the deep end again, laughing. She tries to help Clifford, but both of them are so lubed up, it's no use. "Brings me back to my first Mazola party," hoots Gladys.

Through a slippery series of moves, Clifford makes it to the floor and gets himself standing and collected. He looks at Gladys. "What's a Mazola party?" he asks.

Gladys blushes and hands him a roll of paper towels. "You gonna have to learn that one on your own," she says, winking. Clifford's wiping chunks of grease off his sleeve and pants, wondering if he'll ever get his clothes clean, especially his new shirt.

It's cold and dark in the kitchen, but it's all there. Clifford can make out a grille and stovetop, and there's a dishwasher and refrigerator-freezer, and a slim window with heat lamps looking out into the main space of the doublewide. Gladys has him follow her. Without customers or goings on, the place is sad and empty and full of old ghosts of men and their times.

"This heres the bar, an we got a pool table and foosball," she says. Clifford sees a jukebox, now silent, in the corner. Next to a heart defibrillator is a group of black and white pictures on the wall. "Those is my girls," says Gladys. "Dont be shy. Cmon over and have a look-see." Clifford approaches cautiously. "They wont bite, Cliff!"

There are three photos, each signed in black Sharpie, with little suggestions of intimacy. "Hugs & Kisses," "Be Mine," "Grandma Bugbee," "Puss N. Boots," and "Miss Bunny." Miss Bunny is rather large, and distinctly cross-eyed. "Bunny, shes our youngest. But she left us this past spring," says Gladys. Clifford wonders if this means she died, but Gladys continues, "Moved to Fargo. North Dak. Got a better offer from a womens semi-professional football team. Linebacker." The other two women are clearly more mature. Nature and gravity have taken their tolls, but they still have that gleam, that allure, dressed in their "uniforms." Patent leather spikes, fishnet stockings, satin bikini panties, and diamond tiaras. Puss N. Boots has cat ears on her tiara. "Thems rhinestones in the tiaras," mentions Gladys. "Not the real thing. Everthin else is, though, if you know what I mean." She looks at Clifford. "I see by the way youre studyin there, Cliff, youre kinda interested. Am I right?"

16

"Well, I got to admit…" says Clifford, but he shakes his head. "No offense or anything. They are lovely ladies, but I can't quite go there. Someone old enough to be my grandmother."

"Well, Honey, youre not exactly our demographic. I understand."

"Your girls, they live in the park?"

"Yep, ceptin Miss Bunny."

"I might like to speak with them at some point, if that'd be ok."

"Course it would. Theys all outta work now. Plenty a time on their hands."

All out of work, thinks Clifford. It's got to be a tough existence out here. This place is not exactly the Shangri-La. There's got to be some hardship, and all on top of getting old. Clifford looks around, and notices an odd pink cylinder hanging from the ceiling. It looks like one of those tubes you pour cement into, except it's pink. "What's that, Gladys?"

"Thats our Love Light," she says.

Clifford looks at Gladys and raises his eyebrows.

Gladys is grinning. "Dont knock it til you tried it, Honey." She waltzes across the floor to a bank of light switches. She flips one. Gradually the room is suffused with warm pink light. Slowly it pulsates from dim to bright, dim to bright. Gladys walks back to Clifford and looks to the light, admiring it. "Got a bulb in it with a special tuned frequency so youll feel the Love. Feel the Love, Cliff?"

Two loud thumps come from the kitchen. Then two more, louder. "Oh shit!" exclaims Gladys. "Weaselbomb!"

They hear Big Daddy cry into the vent, "It's you-know-who!" And then it's quiet.

"Shit! Shes the troublemaker!" hisses Gladys. "Keep low!" The two of them get down on their hands and knees and creep over to one of the front windows. Gladys sneaks her head up and peeks out the window. Sure enough, it's Weaselbomb. A thin, high-strung little woman, is practically goose stepping down on Big Daddy, who's standing there, nervously shifting from one foot to the other.

Gladys turns to Clifford and whispers, "She comes off as all righteous an everthin, but that woman is the root of all evil. The Devil herself!"

They can hear the conversation.

"Rupert, whatre you doin here?"

Big Daddy winces and bites his tongue. "Hello Enid, howre you this fine day?"

"Now dont you try smooth talkin me! It wont work!" Weaselbomb had walked right up to Big Daddy and into his space. And if there is one thing Big Daddy needs, it's his space. The big lump of a guy looks like he wants to crawl right out of his skin. "I repeat, whatre you doin here? You know the propertys impounded by the order—"

"Im just keepin an eye on things for Miss Gladys."

"Whys it her car here an not yours?"

Big Daddy's real name (it had to come out sooner or later) is Rupert Twitchit. Or, it was. Four years ago for his sixtieth birthday he legally changed it to Big Daddy. First and last names, respectively. And it grieves him to no end when anybody now calls him by his old name. As he tells it, he'd lived sixty years with that name and that was sixty years too many. He was doing his best to keep his temper. He knew what this pesky, nosey, completely irritating little woman needed—a good stiff poke in the whiskers—but he also knew he wasn't the man to give it to her. Instead, he wanted in the worst way to call her Weaselbomb right to her face. But he wouldn't do that either. He

18

might not be the brightest bulb to come off the line, but he wasn't the dimmest. This little woman's real name is Enid Witzle.

"Gladys asked me to drive it. I offered to use my Jeep but she said no." Big Daddy didn't like to lie. He'd done it, but every time, he knew it just wasn't right. So far, so good for the moment.

"Wheres Gladys?"

"I do not know." This he had to admit was stretching it, but—

"Shes not here?"

Big Daddy looks around and says, "Far as you know."

"Then whys that pink shyster Love Light on in there? Look, you can see it through the window! The Light a Satan, thats what I call it."

"Well Enid, you can call it whatever you like. I spose someone turned it on and forgot to turn it off. I will be sure to mention this to Gladys, soon as I see her."

"I smell a rat," hisses Enid.

Big Daddy thinks yeah, an a skunk dont like its own stink. "Everthins fine, Enid," he offers.

"I dont like it. Im callin the sheriff." Weaselbomb spins on a heel and marches away.

"Have a nice day, Enid," calls Big Daddy. That scrappy little woman, in full twitchy stride, doesn't even turn around. Instead she flips him the finger. Big Daddy sprints around back and hollers into the vent. "Big trouble! Weaselbombs callin the sheriff!"

Gladys is standing on top of the Fryolator with her head in the vent. Big Daddy's booming voice and bad breath hit her like a brick. "Im right here, you lout! There aint no need shoutin at me. We heard the whole thing." She turns herself around and starts climbing out the vent. Clifford wants to get out too, real

19

bad. He needs to pee. Real bad. Big Daddy tries to help Gladys guide her feet onto the ladder, but with his weight on it, it's sinking into the dirt and that top step is a rapidly retreating target. Gladys is worked up and kicking like a mule, which isn't helping any. "Lemme do it! I can do it!"

"Ok woman, ok, just calm down a bit," pleads Big Daddy.

Gladys gets one foot on the ladder and now she's got the other one swinging around, once, twice, just barely missing Big Daddy's jaw. Then she stops.

"Oh God damn it all to hell! Im stuck!"

With his face full of her butt sticking out and wildly wiggling all around, Big Daddy just can't take it and starts to laugh.

"This aint funny! Its my boobs, theys caught!"

"Well Honeybunch," gasps Big Daddy, "we dont want to be hurtin those, now do we?" He's doing everything he can to keep from busting his gut. "How can I help you, my darling?"

"Dont you my darling me!" hisses Gladys.

Clifford, in the mean time, has been looking for a bucket. Or maybe just a corner.

Gladys cries out to him, "Cliff? Where in the hell are you? I need your help, an I need it now!"

Clifford comes running and finds Gladys in a very compromised position. Her bottom half is outside and her top half is inside the small opening, and she's hanging onto the light fixtures above the Fryolator. "W-what can I do?" he asks.

"Its my boobs. Theys caught in the vent. Youre gonna have to help me guide em through."

"Aw, Gladys, I don't—"

"There aint no time for dilly dickin around. Sheriffs comin! Now get up here!"

Sweat is pouring off Gladys' brow. Clifford climbs up onto the Fryolator, which isn't any less slippery than when they were crawling in. With him on top of the thing, he and Gladys are cheek by jowl. "How come you didn't get stuck coming in?" asks Clifford.

"Look, there aint no time to analyze the situation. Now take that one," Gladys nods to her left tittie, "an guide it through." Clifford's about to grab it, but he hesitates and looks at her and she's grinning. "Cliff, havent you ever touched one a these before?" At which point Clifford flushes deep crimson. "You aint!" she squeals. "Aint that the sweetest thing. Now Im warnin you, once you get to touchin em, you might find it hard to stop. But now boy, you understand its strictly business. Theys as nature made em, so dont worry, theres nothing in there to pop."

Clifford takes Gladys' left boob in his hands and gently squishes it and slides it past the lip of the vent.

"Now that werent so bad, was it?" asks Gladys, fluttering her eyelashes.

"No ma'am."

"You did a nice job, nice n gentle. We ladies like that kinda treatment. So now the other one." With both boobs past the lip, Gladys shimmies out. Big Daddy helps her down the ladder and Clifford is right behind her.

"Lets skedaddle!" says Big Daddy. They make a run for the Toronado, jump in and peel out in a spray of gravel.

Back at Gladys', Big Daddy stops the car and they just sit there, quiet as mice, until he and Gladys burst into gales of laughter.

Clifford, in desperation, looks for the door handle before he remembers he's in the back seat of a two door. He cries out, "I got to pee! Real bad."

Gladys turns to him and can see he's in some discomfort. "Oh Honey, Im sorry," she says and leaps out of the car.

Clifford shoves the seat back forward and launches himself out and to a patch of brambles toward the back of Gladys' trailer, and relieves the pressure. It takes a while. Gladys calls, "Cmon in when youre through," as she and Big Daddy go inside. Clifford stands there and pees and pees and pees. He stares out across the open prairie, tawny gold. His thoughts are all astray. This, his first assignment for *The Trumpet*. He had no idea a dynamic career in journalism would be like this. It is dynamic, he'd give it that, but at this point, he simply wants to go home. Clifford steps into the trailer to say his good-byes.

Gladys and Big Daddy are chattering like laying hens in the kitchen. Gladys is a mess, grease stains in every direction. Nonetheless she stands at the bar like nothing is out of the ordinary and mixes cocktails. Three of them. Big Daddy is looking on expectantly as they giggle and yak about the day's events. When Clifford steps inside, they look up and Gladys smiles in a motherly way, "Boy, you look like you been through the wringer," she says.

"Or caught in a grease trap," adds Big Daddy.

"I feel it too," says Clifford. "I've come in to say goodbye."

"Aw, but I was mixin us up a little refreshment," says Gladys. "You sure you wont join us?" She looks at him coyly.

"Thank you, Gladys, but I got to get home. Time to call it a day." He looks down at himself and shakes his head. "But I'd like to come back to continue the interview. I can see this is a much bigger story than I thought. I'd also like to speak with Miss Witzle, in the interest of fairness."

Gladys gives Clifford a hard squint. "That woman, I already told you—"

Big Daddy puts his hand on Gladys' shoulder. "Now Honeybunch, lets not get started. Cliff here has a job to do, after all." Something out the front window gets his attention. "Its the sheriff!" he cries. "Hes even runnin his bubble gum machine!" Brilliant flashes of red light streak through the front bay window and across the living room wall.

The well-worn Police Interceptor slowly crunches into the driveway. Sheriff Dalhart checks in with headquarters on his two-way radio. Leaving the engine and the rotary beacon on the roof running, he gets his clipboard and steps out of the cruiser. His thick leather belt with all the cop gubbins on it creaks, except where his belly hangs over it. He adjusts the tip of his hat and looks around. He's keeping an eye out. He learned from years of experience in law enforcement to keep an eye out, because you never know what you'll see. He walks slowly to the trailer, steps up to the front door, and knocks on it.

Gladys, looking like a horse in a fire, hisses to Big Daddy and Clifford, "What should we do? He gets one look at me or Cliff an hell know exactly what we been up to!"

"Ill answer the door an stall him," says Big Daddy. "You two get into the bathroom an clean up an dont come out til youre presentable." Gladys looks at Clifford, guffaws, and shakes her head. The sheriff knocks again. Gladys and Clifford scamper into the bathroom and Big Daddy ambles over to the door. He opens it and in his most charming, ingratiating way says, "Well good afternoon, Chuck. What all brings you out this way?"

"Good afternoon, Rupert," he says. Big Daddy winces. That's the second time. This just isn't his day. "We had a call from Miss Witzle there was suspicious activity goin on at Mommas. An she said you was there. Is that correct?"

Big Daddy steps out onto the stoop and slowly draws the door closed behind him. The sheriff instinctively puts his hand on his sidearm. "Well," says Big Daddy, "I wouldnt say there was nothing suspicious about it, but yes, I was there. An Chuck, Id sure appreciate it if you called me—"

"Oh. Sorry Big, I forgot. But I got to ask, what were you doin there?"

"Miss Gladys asked me to keep an eye, um, on the place. Just checkin on things."

"I see. An where was Gladys?"

"She's inside." Big Daddy tips his head toward the trailer.

"When you were at Mommas?" Sheriff Dalhart's watching him like a hawk.

A little flustered, Big Daddy again nods toward the trailer. "Like I said, shes inside. Shes just usin the ladies room, an she said shed be right out." Big Daddy looks at the sky. It's one of those crisp fall afternoons on the prairie. The sky's a blue so deep... "Nice fall weather we been havin," he says. "When you think well get the first snow?"

"Soon." That's all the sheriff says. He's not here to pass the time of day. And so the two men stand there, awkward and quiet, and wait. Big Daddy purses his lips, and then smiles when he notices the sheriff looking at him. He shifts his weight from foot to foot. Sheriff Dalhart simply stands there like a stone. A big, don't you even think about messing with me stone. To him, this is way too much to-do about nothing. Men like looking at titties, an some women like showing them off. Been that way since the dawn of time. He likes looking at them too. He stands there, thinking he's glad he's got only 847 days until retirement. Checks them off, one at a time, every day. Not including vacations, holidays, and comp time. Just checking them off.

Gladys comes to the door with Clifford right behind her. All things considered, she's got herself pretty well gussied up. Clean clothes, modest, and her hair brushed nice. Clifford hasn't done so well. He's down to his t-shirt and still has grease stains all over his pants. His hair's combed, but maybe a little more slicked back than usual. Gladys steps outside. Not realizing Clifford's shadowing her like a puppy dog, they get a little tangled up in the door. She manages her biggest, flashiest smile, and says, "Well Chuck, what a nice surprise to see *you*." Gladys looks at him as though she'd like to drag him off to her lair. She is after all a sexy woman, and a woman's got to use what she's got.

"Nice to see you, Gladys," says the sheriff. "An whos this behind you?"

Clifford thrusts his hand out to the sheriff. "Clifford Bagsley, sir, with *The Panhandle Trumpet*. On assignment, sir."

Sheriff Dalhart shakes his hand and notices it's cold. He thinks to himself, holy crap, now they got the press in on this. Whatll happen next? "Nice to meet you, son," he says, and then notices the grease stains on his pants.

"What can I do for you, Chuck?" asks Gladys, giving him a little smirk.

"Gladys, we had a report a suspicious activity this afternoon over at Mommas. What were you doin over there?"

"Oh, you mean just awhile ago?" she asks.

"Yes, Gladys. About a half hour ago. I had a look round an noticed a stepladder round back an the vent hood taken off."

Shit! thinks Gladys. "Well yes… Big Daddy an Clifford here were helpin me with the vent hood. Seems it come off the buildin. Blown off probly. Wanted to make sure there werent no break in or nothin."

"You know the property is impounded, Gladys, an what that means?"

"Yes, Chuck, I do," says Gladys. She smiles and flutters her eyelashes, giving it all the charm she's got.

"You didnt go inside the property?"

"No sir. I didnt."

Big Daddy shifts on his feet, thinking oh, this aint no good. From what I been readin about it, this heres bad Karma. He glances at Gladys, then at the sheriff. Clifford, in the meantime, is keeping a low profile behind Gladys. It's best right now to keep his mouth shut, he thinks.

"Well, Gladys. All a you. Just to be sure, I want to remind you theres no goin in there. Not til this is all over. You understand me?"

"Yes sir," the three of them chime one on top of the other. There's lots of head bobbling going on.

"Then thats it for today. You all have a good afternoon."

"Mm-hmm," says Gladys. "You too, Chuck. Thanks for stoppin by."

The sheriff turns and starts for his cruiser. Like dealin with a bunch a five-year-olds, he thinks. He stops, pauses, and turns around. The three of them are standing there like birds on a branch. He looks at them for a second, then says, "You left that Love Light thing a yours goin. Might want to turn it off next time youre in there." He tips his hat and takes his leave.

Big Daddy looks at Gladys. Her jaw is hanging down. He mutters under his breath, "Might want to shut that thing, before some foreign object flies in there. Insect, or somethin." He shakes his head and goes back inside.

"You sure you aint interested in a little cocktail, Cliff?" asks Gladys.

"Yes, ma'am, I'm sure," says Clifford. "But I would like to come in to get my shirt."

.   .   .

Clifford drives his little Subaru straight home. He has an efficiency apartment in the complex near the post office. He's had enough for one day, and if he walked into the office as is, Mr. Biotte, his boss, would blow a gasket. He pulls the car into his parking space and looks around before he gets out. He'd just as soon not run into any of his neighbors. The coast is clear, so he slinks across the yard and slips into his apartment. He goes straight to the bathroom and looks at himself in the mirror. What a mess! He wonders if maybe he ought to bring some engine degreaser into the shower with him.

After cleaning up and getting into his sweats, he looks at his notebook. It's soaked with grease, and all the pages have stuck together in one solid lump. How is he ever going to make a story of this? It's been a day. He calls his mom.

"Hi Mom, it's Clifford."

"Well, Cliffy, what a nice surprise to hear from you... Everthing OK?"

"Yes and no, Mom. First day on the job. It was kinda rough."

"You want to tell me about it?"

"No Mom, not really." Clifford knows it would be a big mistake to even try to describe the day's events. His mom would be in a conniption, and when that happens, it's never good. "Can you tell me how to get a grease stain out of a shirt?" he asks.

"Is it just a little spot?"

"No."

"A big one?"

"Well, sorta."

27

There's a long pause. "How big of a grease stain, son?"

Honesty is the best policy, thinks Clifford, and hesitantly he says, "The whole shirt, Mom."

After another long pause from his mom, she says, "Soak it in Spray n' Wash. Real good. Dear, are you sure everything's OK?"

.   .   .

The next morning first thing, Clifford shows up at *The Trumpet*. Dick Biotte, editor in chief, waves him into his office and says, "Good morning, Clifford. Have a seat." Clifford sits down. Mr. Biotte is leaning forward in his chair and hovering over his desk. His blotter is a weekly calendar covered with notations highlighted in a rainbow of bright colors. If not for his highlighters, everything would go to hell. He studies the calendar. "Everything go OK yesterday?"

"Yes, sir."

"You didn't show up back here."

"Yes, sir."

"What happened?"

"My clothes got soiled. I figured it best—"

Mr. Biotte looks up at him. "Interviewing the proprietress of a nightclub?"

"Yes, sir."

Mr. Biotte goes back to studying his calendar. "Next time, call, OK?"

"Yes, sir."

"Clifford, what, in your opinion, is the story?"

"About Momma's Little Harry, sir?"

Dick Biotte has been worrying just how he's going to put that name in print, and says, "Yes. That'd be the one."

Clifford puts his thoughts together for a moment. "The story, Sir... the nightclub is an important part of the community at Golden Gardens. It provides a social gathering place, for the men at least, and a livelihood for the employees. And it is unique. It is unclear if complaints lodged against it are valid and of serious enough nature to permanently close it. The business, now closed, may fail before the complaints can all be sorted out. Which, sir, would be a shame." Clifford realizes he's sweating and it's not even eight in the morning.

Mr. Biotte leans back in his chair, squeaking all the way. It sounds as though it's about to fall apart, which is something he never thinks about. He puts his hands behind his head. Clifford notices the underarms of his shirt are yellow and have pit rot. Apparently sweating is not unusual in the newspaper business. Mr. Biotte pouts and looks at him. "Keep on it. Give me five hundred words Friday before five o'clock. The individual against the nightclub, the employees, the clientele. And the law."

"Yes sir, thank you." Clifford is hanging on to the edge of his chair.

Mr. Biotte resumes his hunch over the calendar. Clifford sits still as a post. Mr. Biotte looks up and waves his highlighter in a little circle. "Now go."

Clifford bolts out of the chair and Dick Biotte's office.

Dick smiles to himself and thinks, good kid, glad we found him.

Clifford forgot his notebook in Mr. Biotte's office. Hoping it hasn't left a grease stain on the chair, he scampers in, grabs it, and scampers out. Quietly, he hopes, as a mouse. He goes to the coffeemaker, fills a white Styrofoam cup with the vile-smelling, hot brown liquid, and heads for his desk.

Cathi, the intern editorial assistant from Kansas Tech in Salina, intercepts him, flashes her big smile and blue eyes with lots of eye shadow and mascara, and says, "Good morning, Cliff," in a tone Cliff imagines she'd use if she'd just opened her eyes in bed and he was the first thing she saw and was delighted about it after a night of incredible sex. Clifford freezes. He realizes he's got to stop his imagination because, while she is in fact drippingly *HOT*, she also happens to be not so drippingly *married*, and her hubby is still in Salina.

"Hi, Cathi," he says, barely making eye contact as he moves quickly toward his desk. He sets down his notebook and coffee. He notices the voicemail light on his phone is blinking, so he sits down, sips the coffee, which is pure foulness and wonders about Lily. Lily... Moments drift by. He snaps out of it. Got to snap out of it. He got a "Keep on it" from Mr. Biotte and he doesn't want that to change. He's got work to do.

Clifford plucks at the notebook in hopes of peeling the pages apart. The whole grease-soaked thing has hardened into a brick, and his fingers are shaking. It could be he's had too much coffee, or not enough, or possibly the exposure to Cathi's... to Cathi's *everything*. The ink has run through the grease-soaked pages in every which way. Deciphering what he's written is going to be a chore. The voicemail light blinks. Clifford studies it, realizing it will continue to blink until he does something about it. To hell with the notebook. He decides to call Enid Witzle.

A tight little voice answers, "Speakin."

Clifford's throat constricts and he suddenly thinks calling Miss Witzle may not have been such a good idea. Taking this assignment may not have been such a good idea. But what was he going to say to his first assignment? No?

"Miss Witzle, this is Clifford Bagsley with—"

"I know damn well who you are. What do you want?"

Clifford notices his underarms smell. He looks at his grease cake of a notebook. He takes a deep breath. How can any one woman be capable of striking such terror into everyone around her? "Miss Witzle, I'd like to get your side of the story."

"Oh, would you now?"

"Yes, ma'am." He can hear a cat meowing in the background, and immediately feels sorry for that cat.

"Frankly, Im shocked! I saw you out here yesterday ballyhooing around with those, those… well, I just dont know what to call em." This comes as a small relief to Clifford. He rather enjoyed Gladys and Big Daddy. At least he knows where his lines are drawn.

"Yes ma'am." Clifford thinks he might try being a bit more assertive. "I'd like to schedule—"

"You come out here tomorrow at two oclock, 16 Bluebonnet Lane. Ill be here."

And Enid Witzle slams down the receiver.

Clifford doesn't recall seeing any bluebonnets in the trailer park. Miss Witzle, he thinks, must have killed them all. But OK, 2 p.m. tomorrow, he'd be there. He then calls Gladys in hopes of meeting with her after the Witzle interview, or tirade, as the case might be. And maybe Gladys will be good enough to mix him a cocktail. He figures he'll need one or three by then.

"Honey, am I ever glad its you," Gladys answers. "I was just a little afraid Big Daddy an me mighta not made such a good impression yesterday."

"Not at all, Gladys. It took two whole bottles of Spray n' Wash to get the grease out of my clothes, but they cleaned up. There's a lot of the story I have yet to get. Would you be available tomorrow at three?"

"Id be delighted," says Gladys. "An I promise, itll be just you an me sittin here talkin. No drinkin, no carryin on, no Big Daddy."

"Thanks Gladys, although seeing as how I'll be meeting with Miss Witzle beforehand, I may need a drink."

"You what? Whater you talkin to her for?"

"It's part of my job, Gladys. At *The Trumpet*, we do our best to get the whole story. Nothing to worry about."

"Well, I spose so, I understand. You got to do what you got to do."

"Thanks, Gladys. So we're on for three?"

"Yep, Ill be a waitin for you."

Clifford hangs up the phone and smiles. He likes Gladys. He casts his gaze at his notebook and thinks maybe a plastic knife from the kitchenette would help get the pages apart. And hopefully Cathi won't intercept him. When he gets there, though, she's standing at the counter, making herself a mocha chai.

"Hi, Cliff." She wiggles.

"Hi, Cathi," he says, wondering if her jaw and behind are somehow directly connected. He reaches for a plastic knife from the cup of utensils by the toaster oven.

"Whatcha gonna do with that?"

Clifford thinks he just doesn't want to get into a conversation about what he's going to do with the knife. But Cathi's being friendly and she is a co-worker, so he says, "The pages of my notebook are stuck together." He holds up the spiral-bound mass, adding, "Maybe it will work to pry them apart."

"Stuck together with what?" Cathi smiles at him coyly.

Oh, here we go, thinks Clifford, "It's kind of a long story."

"I got the time."

Clifford fears how open to interpretation this may be, but who knows?

"It's grease. I dropped it in a Fryolator yesterday." Seeing the look on Cathi's face, he quickly adds, "On assignment."

"I hope it wasn't... turned on." If Clifford isn't mistaken, Cathi is starting to blush. "Hot, I mean."

This is all going from bad to worse in a hurry. "No!" shouts Clifford, catching himself, surprised at how that came out. "Not hot. But now all the pages are stuck together in a solid lump."

"You could put it in the microwave for a minute. That might soften it up."

Clifford looks at Cathi. "That's a good idea, Cathi," he says. "Thanks!"

"You bet. Put a couple of paper plates under it." She turns for the door. "Good luck." She looks at Clifford and purses her lips into a smarty-pants grin. Clifford hopes she's not about to blow him a kiss, so he looks away. Or maybe a kiss is what he wants.

But the microwave is such a good idea! He puts the notebook on two paper plates, just like Cathi said, puts it in the microwave, presses the 1 button and then the start button. The microwave hums to life, and he hears his phone ringing. Clifford runs for it.

Back at his desk, he takes the call, then gets distracted with his messages. In the middle of scribbling notes, the smoke detector in the kitchenette goes off. What's that screeching from the kitchenette? What a nuisance! What's the smoke detector going off for...? "Oh shit!" he cries, and runs for the kitchenette. The 1 button, wonders Clifford. Was it for 1 minute, or no, could it have been 1 hour? Mr. Biotte is already there with a fire extinguisher, blasting at the flames leaping from the microwave.

The reek of burning plastic and grease infused with Cajun buffalo wings permeates the air. The sounds of fire truck sirens are getting louder. Clifford stands there aghast, thinking *oh Gawd*, it will be a miracle if I don't get fired before the end of the week. Three big volunteer firemen burst through the door wearing full firefighting gear, oxygen tanks, and masks. They wield heavy axes. They're dying for some action. Fortunately Mr. Biotte has the fire out before they can destroy the place.

After the firemen leave and the commotion dies down, Mr. Biotte has a few choice words for Clifford. But he doesn't fire him. After all, the kid has potential. Cathi thinks it's all pretty hilarious. She texts all her friends about it. Clifford knows he will long suffer his newfound fame on social media.

The next day after going home for lunch—the kitchenette will be out of action for some time—Clifford drives out to Golden Gardens for his interviews with Miss Witzle and Gladys. He glances at the fresh notebook sitting on the passenger seat, and he's determined to keep it that way. On the drive, Clifford enjoys the bright crisp day, the grasses waving in stiff crosswinds. He thinks about how much he appreciates the wide open spaces of the high plains. It's good to get out.

A couple miles from Golden Gardens, he notices a single headlight far in the distance, coming at him and coming fast. It's a motorcycle, leaning into the wind and weaving erratically. With an ear-piercing, high-pitched shriek, it flashes past. Clifford's Subaru lurches to the right in the wave of pressure generated by the bike. He notices the rider is wearing iridescent green goggles and all black leathers. Clifford could swear the guy is grinning. He is big. A big lump. Clifford suspects it's Big Daddy. As quickly as the motorcycle approaches, it is gone, a speck in his rearview mirror. He wonders what all the rush could be about. Is he late for an appointment?

Pulling into the trailer park, Clifford notices the cement block fortifications on either side of the entrance are festooned with pennant flags. They're not real flags, but long triangles of rigid red and yellow plastic with waves molded into them. Whether it's dead calm or there's a tornado coming, they always look like they're flapping in a cheery breeze, but oddly from different directions at the same time.

Clifford feels a tinge of alarm when he sees Betty Carson, the same old woman he saw outside the community center yesterday, out with her candy-apple red walker and heading for the main road. As he approaches, she stops and stares at him uncomprehendingly, but then waves and gives him a big toothless smile. Clifford stops and rolls down the window.

"Mrs. Carson?"

"Why, yes. But young man, how did you know my name?"

"Gladys Calloway introduced us. Mrs. Carson, I hope you're not going out on the main road."

"The main what?"

Clifford raises his voice. "The main road. It's not a good road to walk on."

"I'm fine right here, dear."

"Yes, I can see that. But I'm concerned about the main road."

"The main what?"

Clifford looks at his watch. It's two. "Have a nice day, Mrs. Carson!"

"You too, dear. I'm just out for a walk."

Clifford smiles and waves and rolls up the window. He finds Bluebonnet Lane and parks on the street in front of Miss

Witzle's trailer home. No way is he going to be even the slightest little bit presumptuous, like thinking it would be OK to park in her driveway. Before he can get out of the car, he sees Miss Witzle has the door open and is leaning halfway out of it. She's gesturing wildly with her arm. Clifford gets out of the car and stands there. He waves.

"Park in my driveway!" she screams. "I just hate it when people park on the street! Like Im goin to bite or somethin! Not to mention, youre blockin my view!"

"Hello Miss Witzle. I'm Clifford—"

"By now I know too well who you are! Park in the driveway. *If you dont mind!*"

"Yes, ma'am." Clifford slides back into his car and is tempted as all get out to just drive over to Gladys' and have a drink. But he's on assignment. It's his duty as a professional journalist to get the whole story. So he backs up and just barely misses Miss Witzle's mailbox. Realizing this, he is gripped in a wave of apprehension. Knocking over her mailbox would be just too choice. He pulls into the driveway and shuts off the ignition. He sits there for a moment, takes a deep breath, collects himself, and thinks this must be what the circus performer feels like before sticking his head inside a lion's jaws. He takes yet another deep breath and gets out of the car.

"Hurry up! Dont want to let all the heat out holdin this door for you! Propane aint cheap, young man!"

Clifford reluctantly climbs the steps. He extends his hand to Miss Witzle but she only jerks her head abruptly, compelling him to get inside. "Pleasantries later!" she squawks. Clifford wonders what this woman's idea of pleasantries could ever possibly be. He can hardly wait to find out.

Miss Witzle's trailer home is much the same as any other in the park, but it is neat as a pin. Each piece in the matching

36

living room set is wrapped in transparent textured vinyl slipcovers. Ditto for the lampshades.

"Would you like a cup of coffee, Mr... Mr..." Miss Witzle stands there gawking at him like he just broke into the place. Poor woman probably hasn't had a visitor in years. Sad, but it wouldn't be a surprise.

"Bagsley."

"Mr. Bagsley?"

"Yes, ma'am, that'd be nice." They taught him this in journalism school. If the interviewee offers you a beverage or snack, take it.

"Sit down, Mr. Bagsley." Miss Witzle awkwardly points to the sofa.

"Please, call me Clifford." He notices her shoulders come down about an eighth of an inch. Good! She's relaxing.

Miss Witzle darts into the kitchen. Clifford can hear all manner of clattering around. One sad and scrawny poor excuse for a cat saunters into the living room, slowly drifting right to left as it walks. It's a Siamese. He puts his hand out to it, it gives him a sniff, and Clifford starts to rub it around the ears. Mid-rub, he calls to Miss Witzle, "What's your cat's na—" And the cat, until that moment all slinky and purring, turns on him, spits, and claws him hard, opening up the end of his thumb. "God damn *cat!*" Clifford hisses under his breath while a big dark red bead of blood forms on the end of his thumb.

"Thats Meow Meow," calls Miss Witzle from the kitchen.

Yeah, Meow Meow alright, thinks Clifford. What kind of a name is that? Sort of like naming your kid Talk Talk.

Miss Witzle comes from the kitchen with two steaming mugs of coffee. "What happened?" she demands. Her face contorts with alarm.

"I was patting Meow Meow and..." Blood is now running down Clifford's hand and is about to start dripping.

"What did you do to my poor pussy?" Miss Witzle hurriedly sets the mugs down on the glass-top coffee table with a crash. "Don't get blood on my carpet!"

Clifford is thinking the offer of a Band-Aid might be real nice right about now. "I didn't do anything to..." he grits his teeth, "...*Meow Meow*. She just decided to claw me! Damned if I know why."

"Theres no need to use foul language, young man. Youre makin a very poor impression on the part of *The Trumpet*, I can tell you—"

"Do you have a Band-Aid?" asks Clifford, incredulously.

Miss Witzle, completely flustered and now much angrier than she is the rest of the time, sprints for the bathroom, yelling, "The carpet! No blood on the carpet!"

Clifford watches the blood drizzle down his wrist and seep into the sleeve of his shirt. Journalism, he's finding, is tough on clothes. Does Spray n' Wash remove blood stains? He wonders, he hopes.

Miss Witzle comes back, thrusting a Band-Aid at him. With arms akimbo she demands, "I want to know right now, what did you do to my darlin little Meow Meow to make her scratch you?"

Clifford meanwhile is trying to focus on the Band-Aid. Trying to unwrap the thing, and peel the wax paper off the sticky parts, all with blood oozing out of his thumb.

Miss Witzle stands there tapping her foot on the floor. "Im waitin for an answer."

Slowly and methodically Clifford wraps the Band-Aid around his thumb. He looks up at Miss Witzle and says, "I did nothing to make your... *cat* scratch me. Nothing. Is that clear?"

Clifford is turning red and shaking. He says, "I think it might be best that I leave, Miss Witzle."

"But what about the story? *My* story?"

"Well, I don't know what to say."

"I believe as a journalist you are obligated to get my side of the story," Miss Witzle demands. "An Ive made coffee. Please stay for the coffee, at least." she says.

Clifford can see the woman is extremely lonely. And she did say "please," he thinks, and she made coffee. His temper is starting to fade. "OK. But please keep your *cat* away from me."

Miss Witzle hands him a mug. "Do you take cream or sugar?"

"No, thanks," says Clifford as he takes a sip of the coffee. The strong and foul liquid bites his tongue. Trying not to make a face, he sets the mug back on the table. Miss Witzle takes her mug and sits down in her recliner across the room. Clifford notices her appraising him like a hawk would a rabbit, and is feeling pretty uncomfortable.

"I'd like to get your story," he says. "Why you've sought to have Momma's Little Harry closed down."

Miss Witzle straightens in her chair and clears her throat. "The place, an I make no bones about it, is the den of iniquity. Plain as day." Miss Witzle blows on her coffee and takes a loud slurp. "*An*," she pauses, "they were disturbin the peace. Some of us here at Golden Gardens prefer peace an quiet to that, that... racket."

"How were they disturbing the peace?"

"Carryin on all hours of the night. That sign out front. Pink! With the blinkin breasts! I never heard of such a thing, and so crass! The blinkin light would come in my windows an keep me up all hours of the night. An what they did in there!"

"What did they do in there?" asks Clifford.

"Its indecent!" Miss Witzle purses her lips. "Not fit for polite conversation."

"So it's an issue of morality and—"

"Yes. Indecent. Put that in your story! Heathens! All a them. I just cannot tolerate anythin about it. Livin down the street from blinkin breasts. Pink!"

"What was it like living here before Ms. Calloway opened her nightclub?" asks Clifford.

Miss Witzle hesitates. "I moved here two years ago," she admits. "But still, disturbin the peace is disturbin the peace. Anythin after ten oclock." Miss Witzle sniffs. "Ask Sheriff Dalhart."

"I haven't asked him for an interview. Yet," says Clifford. Miss Witzle sits quietly while Clifford continues with his notes. "So it's disturbing the peace."

"An its indecent! Immoral!"

"I don't believe any laws have been broken in that re—"

"That makes no difference to me, young man! I will not have it!"

"Yes, ma'am." Clifford can see this conversation has nowhere else to go. He looks at his watch; it's about quarter to three. "Well, thank you ma'am for your time and the coffee."

"Mr. Bagsley, have you ever had the Devil live next door to you?"

"No ma'am. I don't think that's possible." Clifford gets up and heads for the door. "Thank you again," he says.

"I hope, young man, you never have to suffer as I have!"

"Yes, ma'am." He turns the doorknob and Meow Meow suddenly appears between his legs. Fixated on the cat, Clifford yanks the door open and stumbles over the threshold.

Miss Witzle screams at him, "Dont let my Meow Meow out!"

"No ma'am, wouldn't want that!"

Clifford has never been so glad to get in his car. With his hands on the wheel he sits quietly for a moment and blinks his eyes, trying to clear his head. He hears muffled screaming. It's Miss Witzle. He thinks she's saying, "You haven't heard the last from me!" He locks the doors, starts the car, puts it in gear and slowly backs out of the driveway. He doesn't dare look back in the direction of the wildly gesticulating Miss Witzle in case she's running toward him with a meat cleaver or something. He thinks what a piece of work, poor woman.

Feeling tremendous relief, almost as good as coming home, he pulls up to Gladys' trailer. Walking to the door, he notices there's no motorcycle sticking out from Big Daddy's tractor shed. That had to be him earlier. Standing on the wobbly steps, he knocks on the door. Gladys comes to greet him wearing a tight-fitting black leotard top and leggings and a short houndstooth check leatherette skirt with a big chrome zipper down the front. Her hair's all poofed up, and she's wearing metallic gold fingernail polish that matches her high heel shoes. She gives Clifford a big bosomy hug. Clifford hugs her back. Get your arms around this woman, thinks Clifford, and watch out.

"Cliff, Honey," Gladys is concerned. "Youre lookin a little grey around the gills. You alright?"

"Yeah, thanks Gladys, but it was a rough go with Miss Witzle."

"I spected as much. Cmon in an well fix you up." Gladys directs him to the comfy chair. "Have a seat. You want a little somethin?" She stands there grinning at him.

"You know, Gladys, I'd love to, but I better not. I've got to tend to business."

Gladys pouts. "Suit yerself. Im gonna mix me a little cocktail. Its the cocktail hour somewhere, isnt it?" She wanders into the kitchen. "Tell me how it went with Weaselbomb."

"Well, I'm not sure who is worse. Her or Meow Meow."

"Meow Meow? What in tarnation is a Meow Meow?"

"Her cat. Pitiful excuse for one. And the thing is schizo. I was patting it and it attacked me. Opened up my thumb."

Gladys pokes her head out of the kitchen. "No! You OK?"

"Yeah." Clifford holds the dried bloody mess of his thumb up for her to see. "Unless it gets infected, I suppose."

"You want a fresh dressin?"

"No thanks," says Clifford as he looks over at the photo of Harry in the breakfast nook. What a cute kid, and what a terrible thing to lose a child. He can't imagine. Gladys comes into the room with a tall Tom Collins and a glass of ice water. She sets the water on the side table for Clifford. He peers up at her with a questioning look.

"Its just water!" she exclaims, grinning.

"Thank you, Gladys."

She plops herself down into the La-Z-Boy with a sigh. She'd noticed Clifford looking at the photo.

"You mind my asking what happened to Harry?" asks Clifford.

Gladys takes a sip of her drink and squints at Clifford over the top of her glass. She smacks her lips and smiles weakly. "Hits the old spot. No, its OK." Clifford sees a subtle wave of sadness come over Gladys, and wishes he hadn't asked. "I was workin at the turkey plant out on the Old Wichita Highway. I did necks an giblets. Id wrap em in paper and then stuff em into the bird before the whole thing got plastic wrapped. Ever day, necks an giblets. Harry would come to visit sometimes after school.

Everbody loved to see him, so cheerful in that Gawd-awful place. One day he was scootin across the loadin yard and got run over by a forklift. Fella was backin up. No place for a child, but no one thought of it. An it was over, just like that."

"I'm so sorry that happened, Gladys." says Clifford.

Fatigue and the old sadness cloud over Gladys' face. "Maybe some good come from it. After that they fenced off the yard, made it safer for anyone might be walkin on the property not knowin the hazards." Gladys takes another sip of her drink. "Then, year later, the place got struck by lightnin an burned to the ground. Felt sorry for all a them birds, thats a hell of a way to go. But the whole town ate roast turkey for a week, free of charge!"

"What'd you do then?"

"Well, I was married, but the grief a losin Harry an then losin my job, it was all too much an split us apart. I drifted around awhile, cryin in my cups. Stayed with my sister up in Michigan, but its just too damn cold up there. She an I were sittin round the table one night an we got the idea for Mommas, in Harrys honor. I came back here. Oklahomas home. Aint much but its home. If we hadnt come up with Mommas, I probly be dead by now."

"How did you get Momma's started?"

"Id been rentin a little place in town. But there was old ghosts, an my ex. An I wanted to get away from the hubbub. I knew bout Golden Gardens, had a couple friends out here, an even though it was an older crowd, I liked it. So I bought this place, on time you understand, an then within a year bought the place where Mommas is. Folks who owned it died out an it was on foreclosure. Id sprung the idea on the girls and they was in. So we picked it up for a song. It wasnt much, but we didnt want much. Needed to change the whole insides all around anyway."

An angry racket from some piece of machinery from outside grows louder and louder. Kind of like a lot of mad bees in a coffee can. It shrieks and pops and gets louder still. Clifford recognizes it as the same noise as the motorcycle made that flashed by him on the highway. It *was* Big Daddy! Clifford cranes his neck to see out the window.

"Oh you never mind him," says Gladys. "Its Big Daddy is all. On that crazy motorbike a his."

Clifford grins. He thinks the motorcycle and the way Big Daddy, who is not a spring chicken anymore, rides it is the craziest thing he's ever seen. He gets up and looks out the window. The noise stops. Big Daddy sits there, legs astraddle the motorcycle, looking like a giant housefly. He raises his goggles onto his forehead and wipes his face with the back of one gloved hand. He's all ruddy faced and windblown. He gets off the motorcycle and pushes it into the tractor shed. Clifford moves back to his chair.

"That's some wild piece of motorcycle," he says.

"Oh yeah." Gladys rolls her eyes. "If he could have sex with that thing, well... anyway. Speak of the Devil, Big Daddy, he helped a lot, put a lot a effort into gettin the place turned around an make it nightclub like. For a share in the place. He an me always been a little sweet on each another."

"That's nice, Gladys."

"For the girls, it took a while for em. I mean, bein older women, the idea a goin topless. Lets face it, aint none of us as pert as we used to be, an I didnt want no falsies, no implants. I wanted my girls to be natural an proud a it. Well, I took the lead an said Id be goin bare breasted, an little by little they came round. Liberatin for us, really. A few people here, both women an men, didnt warm up to the idea. Pushed em a little too far. But once we opened, we sure enough had customers! Little by each over the years, we built it up to what it is today. Kinda proud of a it."

"You should be, Gladys, that Momma's was immediately popular."

"With our customers it was. It aint the vittles theys interested in, Honey, its the *garnish*. You remember seein George an Betty Carson the other day?"

"Yes, I do. I saw Mrs. Carson again today."

"Well they was big on the idea right from the start. Certainly George was, one a the first at our door! An Betty was for it. She helped warm a few other wives here to it, bless her heart."

"Do you get customers coming from town?"

"A few. You got to understand, young whippets like you by an large aint too interested in us old farts. We had a couple curious lookers, but most a our customer base is right here already."

There's a knock at the door, and before Gladys can get up, Big Daddy pokes in his big smiling mug. When he sees Gladys, his eyes widen. "Mm, Honeybunch... you are lookin good." Then he notices Clifford. He sticks his hand in, waves, and says, "Hi, Cliff."

Clifford waves back and Gladys beams. "Cmon in, you big hunk," she says. Big Daddy steps in and fills the room. He's still wearing his black leather pants. He's got suspenders on over a sweatshirt and has a bandanna around his neck. He smells like motor oil and exhaust fumes and he's wearing a big grin. "We heard you on the motorbike. Gawd damn thing."

"Yeah, it was a good ride," he says. "Givin it the Italian tune-up."

"What's that?" asks Clifford.

"A couple blasts to redline. Cleans out her innards."

"I saw you when I was on my way out here. You were moving."

Big Daddy smiles and nods.

"How fast were you going?"

"Fast enough."

"He wont tell you," says Gladys. "Its a secret."

"Let me say," says Big Daddy, "at one time or another I dragged ever bike in these parts an never been beat." His eyes twinkle and he smiles proudly. "How I made my beer money. Used to. Now there seems to be fewer an fewer takers."

"You want a little cocktail, Honeybuns?" asks Gladys.

"Dont mind if I do. Whatever youre havin be fine."

"An I got a little surprise for dinner." Gladys turns to Clifford. "Youll stay, I hope."

"Oh..." Clifford's unsure. "That's really too much."

"Its somethin special. I been hopin youd say yes."

Clifford blushes a little. With the look on her old face, there's no way he can say no. "Well, thank you, Gladys. I'd love to stay."

With this she lights up. She calls a battle cry "*Party!*" and heads for the kitchen.

"Thats a fine woman there," says Big Daddy.

Clifford nods to Big Daddy and calls to the kitchen, "I hope we can cover a few more questions."

"You bet," Gladys calls back. "An after, youll have a cocktail. Loosen you up a bit." She cackles away as she mixes a Tom Collins for Big Daddy and then comes prancing out with the drink. She hands it to him and gives him a kiss.

"Mm, thank you, Honeybunch." Big Daddy puts his arm around Gladys and lets his hand wander onto her behind. He grabs her butt-cheek, gives it a squeeze, and says, "I just love your squidgy bum."

46

Gladys, a little wild-eyed and smiling turns to Clifford, "Whater your questions there, boy?"

"Everything about Momma's is legal? Decency laws?"

"A course it is!" Gladys takes a sip of her freshened cocktail and sits down. Big Daddy sprawls himself on the sofa like a spill of crude oil. He nods his head in agreement. "Mommas," Gladys continues, "is a private club. You gotta become a member to get in. An a private topless joint is one hundred percent legal beagle. All us girls is trained in CPR, an we always keep bottles a nitro tablets in our aprons. You never can tell. An you saw the heart defibrillator, case all else fails. Never had to use it, thank the Gawd amighty."

"What about disturbing the peace?"

"Cept for Weaselbomb, theres never been a complaint. She got a problem with the sign, apparently. If shed be willin to be like the rest a the world, she might pull the shade. You got to understand, most a our clientele are pushin seventy or over. These old boys have gotten over the loud stage. Hell, most of em are on their way home before nine!"

Big Daddy clears his throat. "You ask me, Weaselbomb is just jealous. Nothin moren that."

"Could be youre right," says Gladys.

"What's in store for the future?" asks Clifford.

Gladys looks at the clock, a bit peeved. "Cliff, its almost five. I say its quittin time."

"Just this one question?"

"Well, OK. Thats a good one. We got a hearin comin up next week. But Im hopin to be open again by Christmas. We always done a brisk business over the holidays, plus I dont want to lose my girls. We all depend on the place for our income, or most of it, an they cant hold out forever. Shit, I lose my girls an I lose everthin." Gladys purses her lips and shakes her head. "All because a Weaselbomb." She takes a deep breath. "Look, its quittin time, an thats final, an my surprise otta be showin up any minute now." Gladys snickers. Clifford looks at Big Daddy.

"Dont look at me," he says. "I dont know nothin bout it."

Clifford turns to Gladys, who's attempting to launch herself out of the La-Z-Boy. He looks at his watch. "Well, Gladys, at some point I'd love to meet the girls, if that's possible, and maybe a few of your customers."

"Well, a course. But now, boy, it is *past* quittin time." She gets on her feet and looks at Clifford. "Tom Collins for you?"

Clifford nods his head and smiles. "Thank you, Gladys." Good people here, he thinks. Salt of the earth. And he wonders just what this surprise is all about.

Gladys clatters around in the kitchen and Clifford and Big Daddy start talking motorcycles. Gladys reappears and hands the tall drink to Clifford. She turns, a little unsteady on her feet, and gets her drink. She raises it in a toast. "Heres to Mommas! Long may she live!" Big Daddy and Clifford raise their glasses and call, "Here's to Momma's!" They all drink, they all smile and laugh. They bask in the glow of friendship and whiskey.

Someone knocks softly on the door, and Gladys lights up. She dips her head and hisses conspiratorially at Big Daddy. "Its the surprise!" She sets her drink down and skitters girlishly over to the door, and opens it. "Well, Sweetie Pie, look at you, all so beautiful. Cmon in." Gladys holds the door open.

"Hi, Auntie. Sorry I'm still in my scrubs."

When the young woman steps in the door, Clifford's heart skips a beat. It then skips another two or three. He sits there in rapt attention. "This is Lily," says Gladys. "Shes a dentist... assistant?" Gladys looks at Lily, who smiles and nods her head. "An Lily, this here is Clifford Bagsley." Clifford leaps up from his chair, and the pile of magazines crashes to the floor. Rattled, he tries to pick them up, but Gladys intervenes. "Never you mind bout them. Clifford, meet Lily."

Clifford feels faint as he sticks out his hand.

Lily smiles demurely. "Nice to meet you, Clifford. I'd shake your hand but—" She's wearing mismatched hot mitts and carrying a glass baking dish covered with aluminum foil. She tries to curtsey and says, "I made my special sour cream, chicken, and black olive enchilada casserole. Let me get it in the oven to keep it warm." Gladys leads her to the kitchen. Big Daddy sits there grinning and watching Clifford. Clifford watches Lily.

Her dark chestnut hair is pulled back in a little ponytail. She has grey eyes and fair skin and a matter-of-fact but a little bit shy way of walking into a room. Lily is a beauty, in a farm girl way. Clifford stands there thinking he might need one of those nitro tablets before the evening is over. He turns his attention to Big Daddy, who says in between snickers, in a low voice, "Cliff, you might pick your jaw up off the floor before the ladies come back."

Clifford snaps out of it just in time. He's still standing there in front of the comfy chair when Gladys and Lily come back into the living room. They're chirping at each other like birds. "Whater you doin standin there? A little dumbstruck, are you?" asks Gladys. Lily, who's standing beside her, lowers her eyes and blushes a little pink. She's holding a cocktail, but hers is in a thick glass goblet with a purple parasol sticking out of it. Clifford is staring at the parasol.

"Mine's a piña colada," says Lily. "Want a sip?"

"Oh, no thanks," says Clifford. He holds his drink up and smiles meekly. "I have plenty to handle right here."

"Well, you all have a seat," says Gladys who motions for Lily to sit on the sofa, and then turns to Clifford. "We dont have to stand no more on ceremony, or whatever were standin on." Lily daintily sets herself on the sofa beside the smiling Big Daddy. If ever there was a picture of beauty and the beast, this is it. Clifford, feeling a touch admonished and more than a touch bashful, sits down in the comfy chair.

"Before we have dinner, I thought wed have a little chitchat," says Gladys. "An Lily, Im so happy youre able to join us tonight." Lily nods enthusiastically in the middle of sipping her piña colada. She then wipes her mouth with the back of her hand. Gladys continues, "Cliff, Honey, seems you been askin all the questions. I know its your job an all, but tell us a bit about you. Youre new in these parts, if Im correct."

"I moved here a few weeks ago, after I got the job at *The Trumpet*." He turns to Lily. "I'm a journalist."

"Where all are you outta?" asks Gladys.

"Lamar."

"I just knew it! I knew you was outta Colorada! You got that long Colorada eyesight."

Clifford, not quite sure what to make of this, says, "Thank you, Gladys. I grew up there. My daddy's a pig farmer. I knew sooner or later if I stayed there it'd be either pig farming or the railroad, and I wasn't interested in either one of them. Railroad's going dead, and I had more than enough of the stink of hogs." Clifford takes a good swallow from his drink. He glances at Lily, who's looking directly at him. He's feeling a little exposed. "I don't mind hogs. They're even pretty smart, and I like eating them and all, but I couldn't see a life in it. So I went to High Plains Community College, outside Pueblo, and got my Associate Degree in Journalism."

50

"Then you must know how to call a hog," says Big Daddy.

"I do," says Clifford.

"I'd love to hear you do it!" exclaims Lily, who has moved to the edge of her seat and is fidgeting with the parasol.

"Oh, I'd rather not," says Clifford. "It's kinda loud and all and not—"

"Oh, please," begs Lily.

"Cmon, Cliff," says Gladys. "Lilys beggin you!"

Clifford is turning red. "Maybe later," he says, thinking much, much later.

Gladys turns to Lily. "Hes just bein bashful. Kinda cute, dontcha think?" Lily smiles.

Big Daddy says to Gladys, "Now Honeybunch, if ol Cliff here dont want to call the hogs, he dont have to. Theres none to call anyway, far as I know." He turns to Lily. "Hows it goin at McNultys office?"

"Oh, it's been busy. The big news, even though I'm not supposed to say, is Brenda Dalhart came in with a broken tooth. Poor thing, all upset, thought the olive she was eating was pitted, but it wasn't. She's going to need a crown. Otherwise it's cleanings and fillings, cleanings and fillings."

Clifford's relieved the subject is something, anything, other than hogs.

"Well thats good," says Big Daddy. "Real good." His stomach growls something fierce. "Speakin a real good, them enchiladas are *smellin* real good. When we gonna eat? What else we havin?"

"Cliff, Honey," says Gladys, "sorry if I embarrassed you. Wes glad to have you with us, an some day, maybe when wes outside, Id love to hear a good hog call." She turns to Big

Daddy. "We got Lilys lovely enchilada casserole, an I made a three bean salad an tater tots. An save room for dessert."

Gladys looks up, and whose face does she see peering in the bay window? "Its Weaslebomb!' she shrieks and jumps up from the La-Z-Boy. "Peepin Tom! Im gonna get her!" The face vanishes and Gladys lunges for the door. She sticks her head out and screams, "Weaslebomb! Get off my propty!" Enid Witzle scampers away into the failing light. Gladys turns to her guests. "Where alls my gun? Im gonna get her!"

Big Daddy stands up, straightens his giant self, and pulls up his trousers. "Now Honeybunch," he slowly walks between Gladys and the door. "No sense addin to the hurt already goin round. I seen too much as it is."

Gladys faces him defiantly. She is spitting mad. "Gawd Damnit, I had it with that, that, *weasel* of a woman!"

"I know, Honeybunch." Big Daddy reaches out to Gladys. "Cmon then, lets have us somethin to eat. You just ignore Weaselbomb."

Gladys is still gunning for a fight. "Im tellin ya. I want to settle this!"

"Honeybunch, it aint no use."

Gladys paces the floor. "Well then, lets eat." She turns to Clifford. "We keep it casual round here. We all help ourselves in the kitchen." It turns out to be a tight fit, especially with Big Daddy in there. Clifford can't help but admire the view when Lily bends over to extract the enchiladas from the oven. Gladys notices. She pokes Clifford with her elbow and says to Big Daddy, "The boys already thinkin of dessert!"

Lily turns around, holding the steaming casserole. "Before he's even had his dinner?"

"Apparently so," says Gladys, laughing. Lily looks a little confused, but is more intent on the enchiladas anyway. She pulls the aluminum foil off the top. It's a work of art, what she's done, rows of rolled-up corn tortillas filled with chicken, chopped onions and sour cream, bubbling, with green chile, cheese and, finally, sliced black olives on top.

"That's beautiful," says Clifford, meaning it.

"Why thank you, Clifford," says Lily, beaming. "You've decided to hold off on dessert?"

Gladys snickers, "Not for long, I bet."

Big Daddy admires the dish and sucks his teeth. "Most direct line to a mans heart!"

They all serve themselves from the steaming dishes. Clifford likes standing close to Lily. Gladys has wrapped the silverware in her special cloth napkins with curly fabric elastic bands holding the sets together, fancy like. "Set wherever you want," she calls as everyone exits the kitchen with plates full. Gladys has also put a small arrangement of artificial fall leaves and fruits as a centerpiece on the small table in the breakfast nook.

They all get settled around the table. "Id like to say a little prayer," says Gladys, so they hold hands. Clifford has Big Daddy on one side and Lily on the other. Lily's small hand folds neatly into Clifford's, and his other hand is engulfed by Big Daddy's burly hamhock. Clifford looks around the table and smiles. It feels good to be among friends. Gladys clears her throat and they all dip their heads and close their eyes. Gladys is quiet for a moment, then speaks.

"Thank you Dear Lord for puttin the food on this here table. Well do our best to put it to your service. Thank you Dear Lord for my little Harry, for bringin him to me. Through you, hes brought us all together an I preciate that moren words can tell. An while I cant zactly say thanks for takin him away so early, I spect you know these things betterin me. Amen."

Lily holds Clifford's hand a second longer and gives it a little squeeze. She looks at him and smiles. Clifford smiles back and finds himself blushing. Farm girls, and boys for that matter, can be very direct. Big Daddy struggles unsuccessfully to hold back tears.

"Aw Honeybuns," says Gladys as she reaches over and rubs Big Daddy's shoulder. "Its OK."

"What you say when you say grace," Big Daddy blubbers, "is just the sweetest thing." He apologetically glances at everyone around the table. His big face is red and he looks distraught, but he's smiling. He sniffles. "The sweetest thing... I got to get me a tissue. You all go ahead."

He gets up and grabs a handful of tissues from the box in the living room. Right about the time Gladys says, "Lets eat!" he gives his nose a good juicy honk. Not exactly the best timing, or the most appetizing right next to the dinner table. But no one hesitates to dig in, and in a minute Big Daddy quietly gets himself resituated and down to business.

Gladys gets going again on Weaselbomb. "Im sorry, I just cant help it. I gotta let it out. That, that, *woman!* She come here to the park an it aint been nothin but trouble. She dont have to stay, far as Im concerned. Its like she *wants* trouble. Not happy without it."

"Honeybunch," interjects Big Daddy.

"Please, not now." Gladys has herself whooped up. "She dont have to like my nightclub. Thats her business an thats fine. But now shes comin round to my home. Im tryin to have a nice time with my people, an shes disturbin *that.* I aint gonna have it. Im callin the sheriff!" Gladys starts to get up from the table.

Big Daddy lays one of his hands on top of Gladys' and she calms just a teeny little bit. "Honeybunch," he says, "you know Chuck is probly havin his supper, like us, an he just as soon not be interrupted. Why not we all just have our meal, an then later, you can give him a call." Gladys doesn't say anything, but she isn't getting up anymore either.

An odd and tense moment of quiet settles cloudlike over the table until Clifford says, "Lily, these enchiladas are the best I've ever had."

Lily smiles. "Thank you, Clifford."

"Please, call me Cliff."

Lily nods and asks, "Cliff, how do you like being a journalist?"

Clifford chuckles to himself. "Hard to tell. This story on Momma's is my first assignment, not counting what I did for the school newsletter. It's been... interesting. And well, I met all you folks, and for that I'm happy. Then there's Miss Wit—"

"*Weaslebomb!*" shouts Gladys. "Wicked Witch a the West!"

"Honeybunch, let ol Cliff finish his story," says Big Daddy.

"That's about all I have to say," says Clifford, who then raises his arm to show his blood-stained sleeve. "Although it's kinda hard on clothes."

Lily is alarmed. She leans toward Clifford and puts her hand on his sleeve. "Lord sakes, what happened?"

"Miss—"

"Weaselbomb!" shrieks Gladys. "Strikes *again!*"

"She *bit* you?" gasps Lily, shocked.

"Now Honey..." Big Daddy tries to console Gladys. Again he gently places his big hand on her forearm.

Clifford tries again. "No, Miss Witzle's cat claw—"

"Tried to gawddamn kill him, thats what it did!" screams Gladys.

"Honeybunch," pleads Big Daddy.

"There aint no consolation, Im afraid," says Gladys as she labors to her feet. "Anyone needin anythin from the kitchen?"

"Some more a everthin," says Big Daddy, lifting his plate, which Gladys takes.

"You, Cliff?" asks Gladys.

"Yes, ma'am. Another enchilada, please."

"You can have two," prompts Lily, beaming at Clifford.

"Two enchiladas, please," he says grinning, and hands his plate up to Gladys, who turns to Lily.

"How bout you, Sweetie?"

"No more for me, thank you," she replies. Gladys trots off into the kitchen.

"Poor woman," says Big Daddy in a hushed tone. "So much effort..." He shakes his head and frowns.

Gladys returns and sets the fresh steaming plates in front of the men. She sets herself down. "I pologize for my behavior. Not polite, specially with guests."

"It's OK, Auntie," says Lily.

Gladys leans in to the table and looks around, giving everyone a steely stare. "I been layin on a plan. Time has come to *hatch* it, time for *action*, an Im gonna need help." She looks at everyone and grins. "You all in?"

Each of them is half afraid to say yes and more afraid to say no, so they sheepishly nod their heads. "Tell us what you been cookin up," says Big Daddy.

"The whole legal-beagle thing could take months. Years! Theres a hearin next week, but I aint got months or years. We got Christmas right round the corner, an thats our biggest time. My plan is, we gonna *move* Mommas." Gladys sits firm and nods to herself, quite satisfied with her own cleverness.

"What?" asks Big Daddy. "But—"

56

"No buts. Its a *trailer* home, aint it? An trailers is meant to be towed. We gonna tow it away, far far away from that bit—" Gladys struggles, then snears, "Weas— *Miss Witzle*." She leans back in her chair and places both hands on the table. She means business, and she quietly nods her head. She's got the whole thing figured out. "I been stewin on this. Now the only thing is doin it."

Big Daddy is shocked. He skewers two tater tots with his fork, pops them in his mouth, chews, and thinks for a moment. "Youre right, theys meant to be towed. I guess itd work."

"I *know* itll work!" says Gladys.

Big Daddy leans toward Clifford and says, "Boy, never underestimate the powers of a woman, you hear? Specially a Calloway."

Clifford nods his head. Lily smiles a knowing smile. She, like Clifford, has decided to keep quiet.

"Look," says Gladys, "we got five weeks til Christmas. An frankly, if we miss it, Mommas is done for."

Big Daddy resignedly shakes his head. "Yep," he says, and shovels the next forkful of enchilada into his mouth.

"So its do or die," says Gladys. "I figger I got nothin to lose. We just got to unplug the place, haul its sorry ass a half mile—you know the lot Im talkin bout—an plug it back in. Bingo-bango-bongo!"

"Honeybunch, Ill give you the bingo and the bango. But I aint so sure about the bongo." says Big Daddy, at which point everyone breaks out laughing.

"You old hound dog. You *know* I always enjoy a good bongo," snickers Gladys, and she continues "Well, we all got a lot ahead a us! How bout cherry pie an ice cream for dessert?"

Gladys gets up and plants a big wet kiss on Big Daddy's cheek. Lily smiles and turns her gaze down to her plate. Clifford glances at Lily, then looks out the window.

"Lily, you help me clear the table?" asks Gladys.

"Yes, ma'am."

While the two women hustle plates and pots and pans around in the kitchen, and Lily puts together a little take-home plate for Clifford, the men sit at the table.

"You never know whats next round here," Big Daddy says to Clifford. "Never a dull moment with ol Gladys. Its why I love her so."

"That's pretty sweet," says Clifford.

"What you all think a Lily?"

Clifford turns red.

Big Daddy laughs. "You aint got to say nothing, boy."

"Yes, sir," says Clifford, beside himself, his cover completely blown.

"Whater you two talkin bout?" calls Gladys.

"Oh, nothin," says Big Daddy.

"I got ears in the back a my head," says Gladys.

The men can hear Lily whisper, "That's eyes, Auntie. Ears are on the sides."

"Got them too!" hollers Gladys. She's having a time.

In a moment, Gladys brings the cherry pie and sets it on the table. "I been slavin over this all day," she jokes, then admits, "Its a Mrs. Langfords, store bought."

Lily balances a stack of plates with the tub of vanilla ice cream on top in one hand and in the other is the take-home plate for Clifford. She sets it down beside him. "This is for you. Don't want you wasting away."

Clifford, bashful, smiling, and genuinely touched, looks up at her and says quietly, "Thank you, Lily."

"You give that boy plenty," says Gladys. "I got a sneakin suspicion he gonna be needin it." At which point, Lily turns deep pink. Gladys, chuckling to herself, dishes out the pie and places a big scoop of ice cream on top of each slice. Big Daddy hands the plates around the table. "Cherry pies my favorite," says Gladys. "Hope you all like it."

When they finish with their slices of pie, Lily eyes everyone around the table and says, "Now I want everybody to floss and brush tonight. You all promise?" Big Daddy looks down at the table. "Big Daddy?" she queries.

Ashamedly, he looks up. "I aint got no floss."

"I have some out in the car. Let me fetch it." Lily stands up. "Anybody else?"

"I'm all set, thanks," says Clifford.

"Good here," says Gladys.

When Lily steps outside, Gladys looks at Clifford. "I think I see a little shine bein taken. Pleases me to no end." She reaches across the table and gives Clifford's hand a pat. He grins, even though he's not quite sure what to do or what will happen next.

Lily comes back with three sample packages of floss. She has her arms wrapped around herself. "It's getting cold!" she says, setting the first little plastic tube down in front of Big Daddy. "Now I want you to *use* this," and she gives him a little peck on the cheek. She then gives the others to Gladys and Clifford and says, "Just in case you ever run out."

Big Daddy gets the last smidgen of ice cream off his plate with his finger, and with great satisfaction licks his finger clean. He pushes his chair back and pats his belly. Gladys yawns and says, "I guess we aint the big partiers we used to be." She places her hand on Big Daddy's knee. He's looking a little bleary eyed.

"Time for me to head back into town," says Clifford. He stands up and glances around the table. "Thank you for dinner and all." He picks up the take-home plate and turns to Lily. "And especially the enchiladas."

"Quickest way to a mans, well, a mans everthin!" exclaims Gladys. She shakes with the giggles and blushes.

Clifford says to Lily, "They were delicious. Could I maybe call you?"

Lily rushes for her purse and turns to Clifford. "I'd like that," she says while tearing off a piece of paper and digging for a pen. She comes back to the table, quickly writes her number on the slip, and hands it to Clifford. If ever Clifford wanted to put his arms around a woman, this was the time, but he doesn't know if that would be OK. The two of them stand apart, their bodies yearning.

Clifford studies the number on the paper. He looks up at Lily. "Thanks." In one step, Lily is right in front of him. With great intensity she throws her arms around him and gives him a quick hug. Clifford can feel her strength, her thin body quivers like a guitar string. Just a little bit, she presses her breasts against him, and just as suddenly she releases him. It all happens in the blink of an eye. Clifford is happy and excited. Somewhere in the back of his mind, he knows life is changing, he knows something is coming.

He places the slip with Lily's number on it in his wallet with great care. Then he gathers up his take-home plate, and the floss and his notebook. "Well, thank you again." He turns to Gladys, who's sitting there beaming. "Keep me posted on how I can help move Momma's."

"Oh, you bet," she says.

Lily stands there digging a toe into the carpet, smiling, and biting her lip.

Clifford discovers it is cold out. The ink black sky is a blaze of stars. He looks at them in wonder, gets into his car, starts it, and turns on the heater. Cold air blasts from the vents. He sits there shivering, pulls his wallet from his pocket, and takes out the slip of paper. "Lily" it says in lovely girlish script above her phone number. He feels a little bit warmer.

The next morning Clifford bounds into *The Trumpet's* offices. He's got his notebook and the take-home plate and he's ready to knuckle down on putting the story together. His first assignment, his first real-time published piece, is going to be a blockbuster! On the way to his desk, he notices Mr. Biotte already at work, scratching his balding head, concentrating intensely on something. Clifford just gets to his desk and sets down his notebook when he hears Mr. Biotte say, "Clifford. In my office, please." Clifford notices the voicemail light blinking on his phone, but he sprints for Mr. Biotte's office and stops at the door.

"Yes, sir?"

Without looking up or saying anything, Mr. Biotte waves him in and waggles his finger in the general direction of the chairs in front of his desk. Clifford sits down on the edge of one. The minute he sits there while Mr. Biotte rustles through papers feels like an eternity. Finally Mr. Biotte leans back in his chair and puts his hands behind his head. It's a blue shirt this morning, but it too has pit rot. Clifford hopes Mr. Biotte wears a jacket when he goes to important meetings.

Mr. Biotte frowns. "Clifford, I had a phone message this morning, and then before I could answer it, I got a call from a Miss Enid Witzle. You're familiar with who I'm talking about?"

Clifford suddenly starts to sweat but he doesn't move a muscle. "Yes, sir."

"She is rather upset. Yesterday you apparently assaulted her cat. What's its name?" Mr. Biotte picks up a slip of paper from his desk and stares at it. "Meow Meow?" He raises his eyebrows and looks at Clifford.

"Yes, sir. I mean, no, sir!"

"Please, tell me your side of the story."

"I was patting Meow Meow. The cat was purring and seemed to like it. And then it, the, the… *cat* turned on me, spit on me and clawed me." Clifford holds up his freshly bandaged thumb. "It's a deep wound, sir, and it bled a lot. I have no idea, sir, why the cat clawed me."

"I see." Mr. Biotte glances at his notes. "Miss Witzle also claims you were then a guest at a wild late-night party at Gladys Calloway's residence."

Clifford wants to explode. All this is just so wrong. If there's a way for this, this, Weaselbomb, to take something good and turn it into something bad, she will find it. Exasperated, Clifford says, "Sir, Gladys—I mean Miss Calloway—invited me to dinner after our interview. She and her family are nice people, sir. I stayed for dinner and left. Probably before eight o'clock."

Mr. Biotte nods his head thoughtfully and says, "Clifford, I recognize you are new to town and the profession. It's important for us at *The Trumpet* to give an unbiased view. Because it's a small town, it can be difficult to keep personal and business relationships separate. For the same reason, it can be difficult to avoid being accused of conflict of interest. Is this clear?"

"Yes, sir."

"I'm also acquainted with Enid Witzle." Mr. Biotte, otherwise a picture of professionalism, can't help but roll his eyes. "So I know what you're up against. Please be careful."

"Yes, sir."

"And cats are like that. One minute they love you, the next they're clawing your eyes out. Unpredictable, felines." Mr. Biotte scans his desktop. "That's all for now."

Clifford jumps up from his chair. "Yes, sir."

He's halfway out the door when Mr. Biotte calls, "Oh, and Clifford." Clifford does an about-face and pokes his head back in. "You met Lily Calloway?"

Clifford wonders if nothing is sacred. He swallows hard and croaks, "Yes, sir."

"Nice girl. I'm glad."

"Thank you, Mr. Biotte."

On his way to his desk, Clifford sees Cathi, and calls to her, "Hi, Cathi."

She doesn't even look up, let alone say hello. What's up with that? he wonders, and then he remembers, "Unpredictable." This one he's definitely not going to pat. Once clawed, twice cautious.

Clifford manages to spend a quiet morning at his desk. He finally gets his notes into the computer and starts shaping the story for Friday. It comes around to lunchtime, and just the thought of those enchiladas has his stomach growling.

Although the charred remains of the microwave have found their way to the dumpster, the kitchen still smells like burned plastic, and the ceiling is coated with soot. Clifford's take-home plate is already covered with aluminum foil, so he figures it will be OK to put the whole thing in the toaster oven. This time, however, he's going to stick with it. Nothing will distract him. The plate is warming and a luscious aroma begins to displace the previous days' stink. Cathi wiggles in.

Clifford figures he'll give being pleasant another try. "Hi, Cathi," he says.

She already has her head stuck in the refrigerator, and Clifford's enjoying the view. She pulls her head out and catches Clifford eyeing her. Straightening herself, she is at once pleased and annoyed. "Hello Clifford." Not Cliff, but Clifford. She digs into her brown paper sack and extracts a peanut butter and jelly sandwich.

"How are you today?" asks Clifford, acknowledging to himself that frankly he doesn't care and it may be a mistake to ask.

"I'm OK." Cathi unwraps her sandwich and takes a bite. With her mouth full she asks, "Fwhat argh you cookwing? Psure smalls goodt."

"Enchiladas."

Cathi swallows and says, "I didn't know you were such a cook." She's leaning against the countertop, jutting her pelvis in Clifford's general direction. The pelvis never lies.

"Oh, I didn't make them," says Clifford.

"Then who did? Your mom?"

"No, a friend."

"A *friend*." Cathi squints at Clifford, who is becoming nervous, fearful even, that the claws are about to come out. "Who's that? Wouldn't be Lily Calloway, would it?"

There apparently is nothing that everyone in this town doesn't know all about. Clifford is blushing.

"Uh-*huh*!" mutters Cathi through another mouthful of peanut butter and jelly sandwich. She adds, "*Fyou* sertaghly fdon't wayste andy mtyne!" and stomps away.

Clifford wonders, is there something wrong about meeting Lily? Or just what is Cathi's problem? He hears a sinister dripping, sizzling sound. He turns and is aghast to find smoke seeping out of the toaster oven. His throat tightens. He feels hot. Not again! Please, smoke detector, do not go off! He lunges for the fan switch on the stove hood, hits the HI button, then pulls the plug on the toaster oven and drags it in the direction of the hood. When he opens the oven door, a giant cloud of greasy cheesy smoke billows out, but it blessedly gets sucked away. He hopes and prays Mr. Biotte is on the phone, or in the men's room, or anything other than coming to get his lunch. The smoke detector gives one sharp chirp and then... then... Clifford stares at it. Please! he thinks. And it makes not one more peep.

The oven cools down, and Clifford peers into it. He finds all the smoke was caused by two small drips of goo that had bubbled over the edge of the plate. With a little elbow grease the burned cheese would clean up, and his lunch, the hot plate of Lily Love, is intact.

Clifford is peeling the aluminum foil off the plate when Mr. Biotte walks in. The fan is still howling on HI. He stops and stares at the toaster oven and then looks at Clifford and asks, "What's going on?" He pauses and raises his hands with palms facing Clifford. "On second thought, never mind." He pulls the Texarkana Chicken Chop salad he picked up at Dickie's QuickGo from the refrigerator and walks out. Then he comes back. Clifford holds his breath. Mr. Biotte smiles at him, and without saying a word grabs a plastic fork from the coffee cup full of them on the countertop and again walks out the door.

Clifford takes a deep breath, leans against the counter and quietly savors each bite of the luscious enchiladas, thinking of Lily all the while. She sure can cook.

Back at his desk, Clifford just gets himself focused on the story when his phone rings. He takes the call. "Clifford Bagsley, news desk, *The Trumpet*."

"Cliff, Honey, Im so glad to catch a hold a you. Hower you?"

"Hey there, Gladys. I'm good, and you?"

"Fine. Cliff, we got to have a war meetin. ASAP. Thats soon as possible. Tonight, tomorrow."

"OK."

"An we caint have it here. If Weaselbomb gets a sniff a what were up to, Lord knows, shed find a way to spoil it."

"I can see that."

"Im hopin we can meet at your place or Lilys." Gladys at this point is practically panting she's so worked up. "Could we meet at your place?"

Clifford thinks about this for a moment. "My place is pretty small. But yes, tomorrow night. Tomorrow night would work."

"Hallelujah!" sings Gladys. "Im so thankful, Clifford. Seven oclock be OK?"

"Sure."

"Thank you, Clifford. Preciate it. Look, Honey, I gotta go."

"Let me tell you where I live."

"Already got that."

"OK then. Well see you tomo—" Gladys hangs up with a loud *click!*

Clifford sets the handset in the receiver, leans back in his chair, and stares at the phone. He wonders how soon the whole town will know about this "war meetin." And that he can call hogs, and whatever all. The size of his shorts. He shakes his head. No matter, really, and he gets back to work.

That evening Clifford walks home, and sees a package waiting for him on the doorstep. He notices it's from his mom as he brings it inside. After setting his things down, he opens it and finds a wreath with a note, "For your new front door. It's artificial so you can use it every year. Love, Mom." Before he does anything else, he hangs it on the door. It sure enough looks like the real thing, pine boughs with cones, a big red ribbon and sprayed-on snow. It looks festive.

After dinner Clifford sprawls on the sofa bed in the living room and pulls the precious slip of paper with Lily's phone number from his wallet. He notices part of a list on the back side, "sour cream, black olives, laundry detergent," written in her lovely hand. He thinks of her going to the grocery store, and dreams of how much fun it would be to go grocery shopping with Lily, and about her warmth and good cooking at home. He grabs the phone and calls her.

She answers on the third ring. "Hello?" Clifford marvels at her sweet voice.

"Hi, Lily?"

"Clifford!"

"Yes."

"I was just thinking about you."

"Really? I wanted to thank you for the take-home plate. I had it for lunch today." He then stammers, "The enchiladas, not the plate."

"Yeah," giggles Lily, "I kind of figured. But how sweet. You like my enchiladas?"

"They're the best. Warming them up I almost set them on fire, but—"

Lily starts giggling. "Boys!"

"But I didn't! They were so good. Really appreciate it."

"You're welcome, Cliff. Anytime. Soon, I hope."

"Yeah." Clifford's mind goes blank for a moment. Soon... "I heard from Gladys this afternoon."

"About the war meeting?"

"At my place. You're coming?"

"Yes, seven o'clock. Is there anything I can bring? I'd be happy to."

"Gosh, thanks, I hadn't thought of it." Clifford wonders if he should serve refreshments and, if so, what kind? "I don't know, Lily. I've never entertained before. I'll figure something out."

Lily has already decided she's going to bring a pie.

"You must already know where I live," says Clifford.

"No. Why would I?"

"Everybody else seems to know everything."

Lily snickers. "Small town, isn't it?"

"I'm finding that out. And I thought Lamar was small!" Clifford gives Lily directions to his place. She asks him about growing up in Lamar, and they fall into easy conversation about where they've been and where they're going. And before they know it, it's ten o'clock.

Before they say goodnight, Lily kids Clifford, "I still want my hog call."

"Not tomorrow night, I hope."

"No, but I'm not letting you off the hook. At least not easily."

Clifford smiles. He likes Lily. He likes her a lot.

"You have sweet dreams," she says.

"You too. See you tomorrow."

They hang up. Clifford sits on the sofa bed, holding the phone. Lily wished him sweet dreams. It's only three weeks he's been in town, and already it feels like he belongs.

The next day on his way home from work, Clifford stops by Dickie's QuickGo for refreshments. Once home, after a bite of dinner he switches on the front light. Right about seven o'clock, he hears Gladys' Toronado chugging into the parking lot. He scans his place: he has two lawn chairs set out in addition to the sofa bed, and his biggest bongo bowl full of Cheetos set on the hand-me-down coffee table. He has a twelve-pack of Coors in the fridge. He's pleased. This is his first time hosting a party. The sounds of car doors slamming and general commotion filter into his place, and then the doorbell rings. He opens the door and there's Gladys' smiling face. She's in her winter jacket with a blinking turkey pin on the lapel.

"That's quite a pin you have there," says Clifford.

"Somethin festive, get everbody into the holiday spirit!" she exclaims, and she throws her arms around him. Clifford looks up and there's Big Daddy towering behind her, and beside him, two other women. These must be Gladys' girls, who he wasn't expecting. His living room is going to be some kind of cozy.

As they file in, Big Daddy, who is not the hugging type, extends his hand and says, "A handshakell do." He grins and clasps Clifford's hand in his iron grip. Clifford does his best to cover a wince with a smile and gives it all he's got. Once inside, Big Daddy's looming hulk nearly fills the living room. In come the girls, and amid the clatter and confusion of them all trying to get their coats off, Gladys makes introductions. Clifford has his arms full of jackets and he's wondering where to put them. Over the chairs in the kitchen seems as good a place as any.

"This heres Grandma Bugbee." Grandma is bosomy, shaped like a small pear, and spry. She's wearing a tight-fitting pink cardigan and blue jeans. Her bright blue eyes twinkle, she's got a little button of a nose, and her silvery blonde hair is tied back in a neat bun. At first glance Clifford sees what looks like a nasty bruise on her left temple, but it turns out to be a big bleeding blue tribal tat. He's confounded. Grandma could be America's grandmother. The queen of Crock-Pot beef stews for the family coming over on Sundays. Whatever possessed her to get this big tat, right to the edge of her eye is beyond him. Clifford finds himself drawn to it. He wants to study it but doesn't want to stare. So he looks at her hands. Grandma's fingers are heavily laden with big flashy rings with giant stones, one, a glowing opal is cut like a moon floating on a smoky silver setting.

"An this is Puss N. Boots," adds Gladys as they file in. Round-faced Puss has a worried expression and large, plaintive eyes. She looks like a cat right out of one of those Japanese comic books. She looks at Clifford, silently mimes a "meow," and air-claws at him with her black-gloved hands.

Puss moves toward the coffee table. "Cheetos! My favorite!" she meows.

"I got some Coors, if anybody'd like one," says Clifford. "Gladys?"

"Dont mind if I do." The rest of the gang all nod in agreement, and Gladys continues, "Lilys gonna be here, aint she?"

Clifford, on his way to the kitchen, replies, "I spoke with her last night. She said she'd be here." He pulls beers out of the twelve-pack and gets his collection of football team mugs out of the cupboard, each one with a different team logo on it.

The doorbell rings. Gladys leaps for the door and opens it. "Speak a the devil!" Lily is standing there holding a pie basket. She scans the tightly packed room, and her expression becomes perplexed. "Sweetie, cmon in," says Gladys. "Whatcha got in that basket?"

Clifford pokes his head out of the kitchen. When he sees Lily, and their eyes meet, and their faces light up. "Hi, Lily," he calls.

"Hi, Cliff!" Lily turns to Gladys. "I made a pie, that's what's in here." She opens the lid of the basket.

Gladys takes a good whiff. "Heaven!" she exclaims and then closes the door behind Lily.

Lily notices the wreath. "Lovely wreath, Cliff."

"Aint you sposed to hang it on the outside?" asks Gladys. Everyone laughs.

Clifford turns red. "I suppose—"

"I like it on the inside," quips Lily, coming to Clifford's rescue. "This way we get to enjoy it more." She threads her way into the kitchen and sets the pie basket on the table. She notices Clifford has cans of beer and mugs lined up on his tiny countertop. Smiling and fidgeting a bit, she steps closer to him. "I'm waiting for a hug," she says.

"Oh!" Clifford wipes his hands on a towel. "First, can I take your jacket?"

Lily turns her back to him and he helps her get her jacket off her shoulders. Whoa! Clifford now sees Lily is definitely not wearing scrubs tonight. She's got on a pair of stretch jeans and a tight-fitting orange turtleneck sweater and cowboy boots. And she is gorgeous. Lithe and womanly, she turns and embraces Clifford, putting all of herself into it, and this time Clifford does not hold back. He feels like every part of him is smiling, and so does Lily.

Clifford sees Gladys standing in the kitchen doorway, watching them. Her eyes are twinkling and she's smiling. Lily and Clifford release their embrace.

"What kind of pie did you make?" asks Clifford.

Lily blushes and turns to the basket. "It's an apple pie, and it's still warm. I hope you like it." She opens the basket, and the sweet, rich aroma fills the entire apartment. She pulls a tea towel from over the pie. The top crust has a heart-shaped pattern of little holes poked in it to let out the steam. Lily then pulls a wedge of cheese from the basket and hands it to Clifford. "Apple pie without the cheese is like a kiss without the squeeze," she says.

Clifford, a little dumbstruck, stands there holding the cheese. For a moment everyone is quiet in anticipation. He shakes his head to clear it and asks Lily, "Would you like a beer?"

"Apple pie and beer?" She laughs. "Sure. Why not?" Clifford gets another beer from the fridge as Lily fusses with the pie. "I hope you have enough plates and forks for everyone."

Busy pouring the beers, Clifford points to the cabinet that holds the plates. He turns and Lily's right behind him. They bump into each other, and Clifford just manages not to splash beer all over her. He sets the glass on the table for her, examines the pie and its golden brown crust, and says, "The pie's beautiful, Lily."

"How long we all got to be around this joint fore we get served a beer?" hollers Gladys. She pokes her head into the kitchen and looks intently at Clifford and Lily. "Im just joshin you two lovebirds!"

Clifford feels a little overwhelmed. Lovebirds? *Already?* Guests, beer, Gladys, forks, Lily... his hands are shaking. He manages to bring the filled mugs into the living room and hand them around without dropping anything.

Gladys examines her mug. "Bunnyd like these."

Clifford nervously glances around. Where's everybody going to sit? Lily comes into the room and serves everyone a slice of pie and cheese. It's pure confusion and jabbering, everyone standing around holding on to mugs of beer and plates of pie, wondering where to sit, what to do. Clifford wedges his two kitchen chairs into the space. "Well, everybody, have a seat!" he announces. "If you can."

Big Daddy apprehensively settles himself on one of the lawn chairs. His body consumes it and Clifford prays it doesn't flat out collapse under his weight. The chair creaks and Clifford holds his breath.

Clifford sits himself on one end of the sofa bed. Puss N. Boots settles in next to him, and Lily takes one of the kitchen chairs. Again, she and Clifford's eyes meet, and there's the fire. Clifford so wishes Lily had sat down beside him. With everyone finally squeezed in and settled, they all sit quietly and look at one another. "Would anyone like a Cheeto?" asks Clifford sheepishly and they all erupt into laughter.

"I'd love one," says Puss, who very ladylike plucks a Cheeto from the bowl and daintily places it on her plate.

Clifford is happy to simply sit and gaze at Lily, and find her gazing at him.

Between beer quaffing and pie munching and ooh's and ahh's, Big Daddy leans to Gladys and whispers in her ear, "Nothin says lovin like somethin from the oven." Gladys giggles and shoos him away.

Gladys wolfs her pie, then studies the cheese. She nibbles on it, takes a swallow of her beer, and says, "Everbody, we got to talk business."

Big Daddy nods as he stuffs the last bite of pie into his gaping maw. He holds up a finger. "Lily? Are there seconds on pie?"

"Two pieces left. One's for Clifford's breakfast," she says, smiling demurely.

Big Daddy looks around the room, happy to see there don't seem to be any other takers. "Id be happy to have the other one then."

Lily gets up and reaches for Big Daddy's plate. "What about me?" cries Gladys.

"Honeybunch?" Big Daddy looks at her, concerned. He wants that pie.

She pokes him with her elbow. "Its for you, Honeybuns."

Lily takes Big Daddy's plate into the kitchen. Clifford gets the remaining beers from the fridge and sets them on the coffee table. "Seconds on beverages are self-serve," he says. Big Daddy gets up, grabs one of the beers, and plops himself down again with a loud crunch from the chair. Again, Clifford holds his breath.

Lily returns and hands Big Daddy his seconds on pie. He looks up at her and smiles. "Thank you, darlin."

"Everbody set?" asks Gladys. She scans the faces in the room, and says, "Now to business. We got three things to worry bout. One, unpluggin Mommas from where she is now. Two, pluggin her in to her new digs. An three, doin what needs to get done here in town. Well, an we got movin her an this an that. Anyhow, I figger me an Big Daddy can take care of the unpluggin and gettin her ready to roll, Grandma and Puss here can take care a making sure the new site is all hunky-dory, an you, Clifford an Lily, can help with things needin to get done here in the village. I can yickety-yak on the phone all I want, but there aint no replacin a little face to face for gettin things done." Gladys pauses and purses her lips. "Done is one a my favorite words."

"You have permission from the trailer park to do this?" asks Lily.

"Uh-huh," says Gladys. "Talked to the manger, an he says one patch a prairie or another, makes no difference to him. Rents all the same."

"What is it we can do in town?" asks Clifford.

"Gettin Angel on the ball. Hes got a towin service. An maybe runnin stuff we might need out to the park. An coordinatin with us, pluggin out an pluggin in. Bingo bango bongo!"

Big Daddy starts chuckling, and his belly bounces with a life of its own. "I just love the way you say that, Honeybunch." He nibbles down the last morsel of his pie, then chases the crumbs around the plate with his finger. He also loves just how naive Gladys is. Nothing out at Golden Gardens is bingo bango bongo. Especially anything vaguely resembling moving. Gladys throws an approving look at Big Daddy who is now picking up the last little smidgens off his plate. Satisfied he has them all, he puts his finger in his mouth, licks it clean, and then pulls it out, making a loud POP! "Mm-*MM!* Sure do love your pie, Lily."

Lily smiles. "I'm glad you do," she says.

"Anybody got any questions?" asks Gladys. She places her hand on Big Daddy's knee.

"What bout the new site?" asks Grandma. "Clearin brush an what all."

"Hadnt thought a that," says Gladys. "Why dont you girls see what you can figger out."

This is the first of what seems to Gladys will be a hundred questions. It goes on and on until finally everyone, and Gladys especially, is pooped.

"Gladys, let me give you my email," says Clifford.

"Me? Honey, I aint got no fool computer. I just let my fingers do the walkin!" Gladys tiptoes her fingers up Big Daddy's thigh.

Big Daddy yawns and grins. "*I* think its time to go home."

No one needs any further encouragement to call it a night. They all get up and awkwardly mill around and bump into one another while Clifford gets all the jackets from the kitchen. Lily gathers dishes and quickly piles them high the kitchen sink.

Being a gentleman, Clifford tries to help the women get their jackets on. Arms and elbows swing in every direction as they all try not to punch one another in the eye. Hugs and thanks go around, and Clifford just gives Big Daddy a wave. His hand just isn't up for another crushing.

They all file out, Clifford stands in the door watching them pile into the old Toronado. It's a fire drill in reverse. He waves, and closes the door. He can hear Lily in the kitchen, washing dishes and whistling a tune. Her presence makes him comfortable, gives him a warm feeling. He walks into the kitchen. "Really, you don't have to do those," he says.

Lily looks up at him. "Oh, I'm happy to. It's kinda taught into me."

Clifford picks up a towel. "At least then, I'll dry." They work in the kitchen, quietly enjoying the easiness of being together. Lily puts the last piece of pie and cheese on a plate and gathers up her basket. When she finishes, she plants herself on one end of Clifford's sofa bed, smiling, with her hands folded in her lap. "Is there anything I can get you?" asks Clifford from the kitchen.

"I'm good, thanks."

Clifford walks into the living room and stands there for a moment. He's been wanting to get cozy with Lily all evening, and now that he has his chance he finds himself more than a little nervous. What happens now? Should he sit next to her? Close to her? Put his arm around her? Or sit on one of the chairs? He has no idea, so he takes a chance and sits down beside her, close but not too close. Lily leans toward him. "How was your day at the paper?" she asks.

When Clifford answers, he leans toward Lily. "It was good."

Lily rearranges herself a little closer. "You're working on the story about Momma's?"

"Yes," says Clifford. "Almost finished with my first installment." He skooches toward Lily a quarter inch. "It's going to be quite a story."

"I bet. Auntie Gladys, she's a hoot, isn't she?" Lily turns so her knee brushes against Clifford's thigh. "And what all happened with the enchiladas? You almost set them on fire?"

Clifford jumps up. "I almost forgot your take-home plate! Let me get that for you." He leaps into the kitchen, pulls the plate from the shelf, and places it on Lily's pie basket. He turns to her and asks, "This OK here?" and notices she's now sitting in the middle of the sofa bed.

"That's fine," she says and puts her hand on the cushion next to her. She gives it a pat. "What all happened in the kitchen? At work, I mean."

Clifford sits so he's facing Lily. "It's a little embarrassing."

"It's alright. I won't laugh."

"Well…" Clifford recounts his fat-soaked notebook disaster, and Lily sits there doing her best not to laugh. She's turning red and struggling to contain herself. Clifford notices. "You think it's funny?" At which point Lily bursts into laughter, and tears stream down her cheeks.

"Keep going!" she squeals. Clifford's sitting there looking forlorn. "Oh, Clifford," says Lily. She puts her hand on his thigh. "I'm sorry. I said I wouldn't laugh." And she starts laughing again, uncontrollably, "But it's so," she gasps, *"funny!"*

In all of Lily's delight, Clifford can't help but join her. He gets laughing some more and tries to continue with his story, but it's no use. As soon as the two of them calm down, they glance at each other and it starts all over again. Clifford puts his hand on Lily's knee. Using her sleeve, Lily wipes the tears from her eyes.

"Oh, Clifford, that is such a great story. I hope you'll write it down."

"I'm not sure *The Trumpet* would be interested."

"No matter. It's just too good."

"Well, thank you."

Lily leans over to kiss Clifford. She gets a couple inches away and stops. She looks into Clifford's eyes and smiles. He smiles back, closes the distance, and they kiss. That first soft, tentative little kiss. Both of them are feeling waves of a very special warmth, and they kiss again, this time lingering. Clifford backs away. "I... I've never done any of this before."

Lily looks away and blushes a little. She squeezes Clifford's hand, turns her gaze back to his, and whispers, "Neither have I."

.   .   .

The morning comes up cold and grey, and a biting north wind bears down on the prairie. TV antenna guy lines send a lowing hum through the roof of Gladys' trailer. The louvered glass in the front door rattles. Gladys is up, but Big Daddy is still in bed. She pads around in her robe and slippers, as she looks for her hat. Damn that wind, she thinks. It sucks the heat right outta the place. She jacks up the heat another notch, thinking to hell with what propane costs, and gets coffee started. She finds her hat, pulls it on, and grabs the afghan. The coffeemaker gurgles and wheezes. She sets herself in the La-Z-Boy, tucks the afghan around her legs, and looks at the photo of Harry.

The heater rattles and buzzes and slowly the place warms up. Gladys is just about to snooze off again when the coffeemaker lets go its last surging gasp and then is quiet.

Coffee's ready, and it smells some kind of good. Gladys struggles to get herself out of the La-Z-Boy, shuffles into the kitchen, and pours two cups. She watches tendrils of steam rise and disappear. The yellow smiley-face mug is for Big Daddy. Mornings, he needs all the help he can get. He's a lump of a grump, Gladys thinks to herself, chuckling. She takes the mug into the bedroom and sets it on the bedside table. She can see Big Daddy's nostrils twitch. He's sniffing it. Slowly, he opens one eye. A little smile creeps over his bristly face.

"Mornin, you old lump," says Gladys as she pats his big hind end rising up under the covers.

"Mm, Honeybunch, you treat me so good," says Big Daddy.

"Cold an grey this mornin. An winds a whistlin," says Gladys.

"Why dont you come on back to bed for a little visit?" mumbles Big Daddy. He turns his one open eye up to Gladys. She's looking down on him, thinking how much that one glazed eye peering up from his bulk resembles that beached whale she saw a picture of in the nature magazine at Dr. McNultys office. She laughs. "What so funny?" he mumbles.

Gladys gazes down at her man. She just loves him to pieces. "Aw, I was just thinkin."

"Bout what?"

Gladys giggles. "Bout how much you look... how much you look like a beached whale."

Big Daddy buries his face in the pillow. Muffled, he says, "First thing in the mornin, thats a hell of a thing to say to a feller!"

Gladys pats his shoulder. "I got to get my coffee before it gets cold."

"You not comin back to bed?"

Gladys calls from the hallway, "Naw, we got a busy day before us. You get up." She hears Big Daddy groan. Back in the kitchen Gladys sips her coffee. Hot, black, and bitter, just the way she likes it. She peers out the window over the sink. A tumbleweed blows by in the greyness. Hell of a day, thinks Gladys, looks like snow. The coffee helps push the dreariness of it all back a bit. She looks in the fridge, rummages around, pulls out a carton of eggs and a package of bacon, a loaf of bread for toast and the jar of grape jelly. The tub of oleo. They're going to need a breakfast with staying power.

Big Daddy ambles into the kitchen in his skivvies, while Gladys still has her head in the fridge. He gently places his hands on her hips and presses himself into her ample behind. "Mm, now Honeybuns," says Gladys and she swats at him, "dont you be a *bad* boy. Now you stop it." Yet she presses herself back into Big Daddy.

"You sure you dont want a little visit?" coos Big Daddy.

"Honeybuns, you know I would, but," Gladys straightens up, "we got mountains before us." Gladys turns to Big Daddy and gives him a peck on the cheek and a pat in the trousers. "Maybe save some for tonight?"

"Oh, awright, I know, we gots lots to do." He looks out the window. "Damn, what a miserable day. It just aint fit fer man nor beast."

"Cmon you old sluggabug," says Gladys. "Help me get some breakfast started."

"If were not gonna be visitin, lemme get dressed," Big Daddy calls as he heads for the bedroom. "Be right back."

Gladys starts peeling strips of bacon out of the vacuum pack and lays them in the skillet. Six strips each ought to be enough. It starts sizzling and popping and smelling real good. Big Daddy returns, dressed in his coveralls, his hair still all over the place, wisps going every which way. Gladys takes one look at him, smiles and shakes her head.

"Whats so funny now?" asks Big Daddy.

Gladys puts her arms around him. "Theres times I see you an know just how you were when you was six. I can just see it." She kisses him on the cheek, thinking one of the things so sweet about men is how much they're just big overgrown boys. Of course every woman knows this can also be the most irritating. "You could get some plates out, an put bread in the toaster," she says. Big Daddy refills Gladys' mug and then his own, then reaches for plates.

There's a knock at the door. Gladys strains to see the clock. It's only twenty past seven. "At this hour?" she says. "Better not be—" She sets down her mug, wraps her robe closer around her front, snugs up the belt, and goes to the door. "Who is it?" she calls.

"Bill Dukish." and another voice, "Its Sam." Two of Gladys' customers.

Before opening the door, Gladys glances back and sees Big Daddy peering out of the kitchen. Gladys raises her eyebrows. "Dont know what it could be. You tend to the bacon." She opens the door. The two men are standing there in their insulated coveralls, and holding their hats. Sam's coveralls are fitting pretty tight around his belly, a belly that probably wasn't there twenty years ago when he was a working man. "Good morning, gentlemen," says Gladys.

"Mornin Miss Gladys," says Bill.

"Everthin OK?" With their sincere old faces looking up, they smile and nod. The first few spits of snow stream by. "Whynt you come in so were not standin here, you freezin an me lettin all my heat out," says Gladys and she steps aside. The two men eagerly climb the stairs and crowd in.

"Mornin Bill, Sam," says Big Daddy.

"I bet these fellersd like a cup a coffee," says Gladys. "Honeybuns, would you make another pot?"

"Yep," calls Big Daddy.

Gladys turns to her guests. "Bill, Sam, what alls the nature of your visit?"

Sam says a little sheepishly, "Me an Bill, well, we heard from Miss Boots you be needin help with Mommas. Movin an all."

"Word does get round, dont it?"

"Yes maam."

"Bill here, if you dint know, is a certified electrician," says Sam. "An I was a plumber. Well, I worked in the steam plant at the hospital in Tulsa. That was 1963—" Bill nudges him with his elbow. "Anyway, we know youll be needin electric an plumbin help, so here we is."

Big Daddy hands the men steaming mugs of coffee. Right away, before it's cooled, they take big gulps. "Whynt you gentlemen take a load off," says Gladys. The two of them crowd onto her little love seat. Big Daddy returns to the kitchen.

"You hear right. Well be needin help." Gladys picks up her mug, sips her coffee, and thinks for a minute. "Whatin you charge? I dont got much money."

The men glance at each other. "We already got our pay," says Sam.

"By who?" asks Gladys, a little confused.

"Why, you an the girls," says Sam. "What you all done for us, for everone here. We been missin Mommas an we want to see her come back. Theys be no charge for what we do."

"We mightin not be fast as we used to," says Bill. "But wes sincere. We kin get the job done an get it done right."

"An Ol Man Brucey, he wants to help too," adds Sam. "He dont got no trade, but he can help with just about anythin."

Big Daddy returns from the kitchen and stands beside Gladys, who says, "I got to pay you gentlemen somethin. Aint right to have you workin for free."

Bill and Sam exchange glances. Bill purses his lips. "Nope."

"I got to."

"A beer then," says Bill.

"Yep, a beer." says Sam. "Thatd be good. One each, that is."

"You drive a hard bargain," says Gladys. The two men unceremoniously stand up. Gladys is touched. "I cant tell you how preciative I am," she says. "Really preciate it."

"Thank you for the coffee, Miss Gladys," says Bill.

"Youre welcome. When can you start?" asks Gladys.

"Right now," says Sam. "We got tools outin the truck. But smells like you an Big Daddy got bacon to eat."

"Lets meet at Mommas in forty-five minutes. Sound good?" says Gladys.

"Yes maam. Well gather up Ol Brucey in the meantime," says Bill as he and Sam take their leave.

Big Daddy has the bacon out of the pan and is cracking six eggs, one after the other, into the pool of hot fat left behind. Gladys walks into the kitchen. "Aint that nice bout Bill an Sam, they helpin us."

"You got friends, Honeybunch."

The eggs bubble and spatter. Big Daddy splashes hot fat over them with the spatula to cook the tops. "I love when my man does the cookin," says Gladys.

Big Daddy assembles the plates and Gladys spreads oleo and grape jelly on the toast. They take their plates to the table, and sit down. Gladys says a little grace and then, "Lets eat." They set to it and discuss the day ahead.

Bill and Sam are waiting in Sam's truck at Momma's by the time Gladys and Big Daddy get there, and they get out when they see the Jeep come wheeling up. It's some kind of cold with snow still spitting in the wind. "Hope this storm holds off," calls Gladys. "Lets all get on the downwind side," she adds.

Loose bits and pieces of the doublewide clank and rattle, so does the satellite dish cable that comes off the roof, and the glass in the windows. They all head for the far end of the trailer. "We went by Ol Bruceys place but he werent round, not hide nor hair a him," says Bill.

"Thats OK," says Gladys. "Just so you know, we aint sposed to be goin inside Mommas long as shes impounded by the sheriff. That shouldnt be no problem. What all we gotta do, we can do from her undersides. Nice little crawl space underneath. Outta the weather, too." Gladys yanks at a loose section of the corrugated skirting, which makes horrible screeching and chafing sounds in the brambles. The men stand and watch. Over the years they've learned when Gladys sets to do something, it's usually best to let her alone. She pulls and strains and cusses and the skirt gives way. She stands back, admires her work, and catches her breath. "Be my guest," she says in a way only Gladys can, coquettish in coveralls, and directs the way for the men to crawl under the trailer. Each of them takes out his flashlight and turns it on. They're prepared.

It's all dust and dirt and bad smells, and there's just enough room for them to inch around on their bellies. "Nice to be outta the wind," says Big Daddy. He turns to Gladys in the murk. There's no hiding his grimace, but he adds, "Always think postive."

"Damn glad its past rattler season," says Gladys.

"You sure?" asks Bill, alarmed.

"Think so," says Gladys.

"Think sos the best you got?" asks Sam. Gladys nods.

Bill stops moving. Slowly, with eyes wide, he turns his head to look at Big Daddy and Gladys. "Rattlers?"

"Dont you worry, theys past." reassures Big Daddy.

Crawling around, despite moving slowly, they stir up clouds of fine dust. The flashlight beams flicker in it, and it clings to spiderwebs, which are everywhere. Gladys starts coughing. "How bout black widows an brown recluse?" asks Bill.

"Theys past too. Nothin to worry bout," says Gladys.

"Damn glad it aint July," grumbles Sam.

A scratchy and all too familiar voice calls from outside, "Hel-lo?"

Gladys snaps up and hits her head on a floor joist. "God damn it," she hisses. She knows the voice without looking. "Its Weaselbomb!"

"Hel-lo?" Gladys spits into the dirt. It's the most irritating, grating, weasely voice she's ever known. "Cant that woman leave us be?"

Big Daddy winces. He knows whatever's going to happen, it is not going be good.

"Who alls in there?"

Gladys hisses at Big Daddy, "Lemme have your flashlight." She grabs it before he can say yes or no and shines the beam in Weaselbomb's face. "What all do you want?"

"Is that you, Gladys?" Enid screeches, her beady little eyes blinking in the glare.

"Yeah its me. What you want?"

"You arent sposed to be havin anythin to do with this place. Im callin Sheriff Dalhart!"

Gladys shimmies toward Enid, equal parts soldier keeping low under enemy fire, and freight train. She's thinking it's high time to have it out. Enid stays put with her head poking into the opening. "Move over! Im a comin out!" growls Gladys.

Sam turns to follow Gladys, but Big Daddy holds him back, muttering, "Gonna be a catfight. Best keep clear."

Gladys gets out from underneath the trailer. Covered with dirt and spiderwebs, she rises up in all her mightiness and puts her clenched fists on her hips. Only a fool would mess with her.

Enid takes a step back and swallows. She swallows hard. "Now, now, Gladys. Please dont do nothin youll regret," she squeaks. Enid points at the front door. "You know the sign says—"

"I know what the goddamned sign says!" bellows Gladys. "It says no entry. Well, we aint entrin! So why dont you take your scrawny little ass an move it outta here, for I kick it clear the next county!"

Enid, shocked, takes another step back. "Whatre you doin in there?"

Gladys takes a step forward, closing the gap. "Maintnence! Wes preparing for Mommas Grand Reopening! Sign dont say nothin bout maintnence now do it?"

"Well, I—" Enid cocks her head. "Reopening?"

"Why dont you git?" Gladys takes another step toward Enid and stamps her foot in the dirt. "Git!" Enid backs off and this continues, one step at a time, until Enid's backed herself into the driveway. All the while she's been thinking, reopenin? How could this be? They havent even had the hearin yet.

The snow's coming down now like it means it. Gladys curses the sky. She lowers her gaze to Enid's pale little face, slowly raises an arm, and points a finger toward the street. She growls low and mean, "Off my property, Enid Witzle." Gladys stares into Enid's eyes. "Crimnal trespass is what this is." She sees fear there, and for an instant, Gladys feels bad. She doesn't like this at all but she continues. "You git off. *Now!*"

Enid backs away and when she gets to the street, she stops. She raises a tiny shaking fist, and screeches, "This aint the last of it!" She turns and scurries, disappearing into the driving snow.

Gladys stands there for a moment, panting, trying to collect herself. She doesn't like seeing fear in people. That isn't what Momma's Little Harry is about. Not at all. Feeling shaken and low, she walks back to the trailer and crawls under it.

Big Daddy sees her, knows her troubles, and reaches out. "You OK?"

"*No!*" hollers Gladys and she breaks down and blubbers, "I need a hug."

Big Daddy tries to sit up and hits his head with a good loud *thunk.* "Good thing that werent one a my sensitive parts," he says, putting an arm around Gladys as best he can and giving her a squeeze.

Sniffling, Gladys says, "You fellers know what to do morin me. Im goin home. Gotta call Angel."

"Want a ride?" asks Big Daddy.

"Thank you, Honeybuns, but a walkll do me good. You all come back when you need a coffee break."

Gladys crawls out from under the trailer. Snow is coming down fine and hard, and the wind has turned westerly. She pulls her hat over her ears and walks toward her trailer. It's only three lots away, but she can't even see it. The cold bites at her face. She peers into the driving snow, and thinks about the stories of people getting lost in whiteouts and dying from the cold. Sometimes they wouldn't be found until spring. That's the prairie in winter. She picks up her step and follows the road while she can still see it.

Back in her trailer, she peels off her wet, filthy coveralls and hat, goes into the bathroom, and washes up. The upwind side of the trailer is already coated in snow. She can't see out the windows. The place creaks and rocks in the wind. She makes another pot of coffee for when the men get back. The kitchen window is the one little view beyond all her troubles where she can still see out. Gladys watches the snow for a moment and feels despair. Sure do hope this blows through, she thinks. A big snowfall would put the kibosh on her plans, and to Momma's. "Where theres a will, theres a way," she mutters to herself as she turns and looks in the freezer to see if maybe she has some sweet rolls. There's the ham she got on special right after Easter she's saving for Thanksgiving, but no sweet rolls. Menll have to do with toast an jelly, if they want, she thinks.

When the men get back, they have Old Brucey with them and he's soaked to the bone. His cobbly old teeth are chattering, but nothing can defeat the twinkle in his eyes. "Good morning, Gladys," he says, shuffling in as though nothing is out of the ordinary.

Alarmed at his appearance, Gladys demands, "Brucey, where you been?"

"We found him at the new lot," says Big Daddy, "clearin brush."

"Brucey! In the snow?" Gladys is shocked, and more than a little worried for the old geezer.

Old Brucey just smiles and collapses in a chair. "Miss Boots spoke to me this morning," he says in his thick Hungarian accent. "I was out getting my paper, and she told me what was going on and said you needed help. Thought I better get as much of that brush as I could before the snow settles in."

Gladys looks at Big Daddy. "How much he get done?"

"Bout half the lot," he says.

"I just don't have the get-up-and-go I used to," says Old Brucey. "Back in my time, I'd have the whole thing clear."

Gladys shakes her head. "You are somthin, you Old Coot. Get outta those soakin coveralls an lemme get you some coffee." She comes back with four steaming mugs. "I aint got no sweet rolls, but I can make up toast an jelly."

"Aw, naw, thats OK," says Bill in his bashful way. "We dont wanna be no bother."

"Aint no bother at all," says Gladys as she turns for the kitchen. She makes another pot of coffee, then toast, and slathers on plenty of oleo and jelly. She takes a plate out while the coffeemaker groans away. Four worn and eager hands grab into the toast. She knew her men would be hungry. Gladys lowers herself into the La-Z-Boy. "Brucey, sure am preciative a what you done," she says and looks at the men. "All a you. I cant tell you what your help means to me.

"The least we can do, Miss Gladys," says Old Brucey enthusiastically through his mouth full of toast. Crumbs and spittle spray onto his lap.

"You get ahold a Angel?" asks Big Daddy.

"Nope. No answer. Youd think he might get a ansrin machine one a these decades."

"If he did, hed just break it," says Big Daddy. "Just as well."

"Ill call Cliff. Maybe he can stop by on him."

.   .   .

Clifford's at the newspaper when Gladys calls. A load of other assignments is piling up on him. He needs to get out and do interviews, but he's using the snow as his excuse to stay put.

The deadline for his first installment of Momma's story is less than a day off, and he doesn't have a whole heck of a lot down. After last night he's a little distracted. He seems only to think about Lily, that first tantalizing kiss, and everything else.

He picks up the phone.

"Mornin, Cliff. Its your Auntie Gladys."

Clifford is jarred from his daydream. "Gladys? Auntie?"

"Well yeah, seeinz how were nearly family. You get any sleep, nephew?"

"Um, nephew? Yes ma'am, Gladys. And you?"

"Now dont be a smartypants with your elder. Clifford, I need your help."

"Sure. What can I do?"

"Can you stop by Angel Mahoneys? I tried callin but no answer. Dont mean nothin."

"Angel Mahoney?" asks Clifford.

"Yep. He runs a towin service. Im hopin hell tow Mommas."

"Where is he located?"

"Just bfore you get to the turkey plant, whats left of it. Out Old Wichita Highway. We gotta get him lined up for the move."

"This afternoon be OK?"

"Thatd be lovely, thank you. An Clifford, that was real nice a you havin us over last night. Means a lot to me. Preciate it."

"You bet."

"An I noticed Lily dawdlin behind. You two lovebirds have a nice evenin?"

"Yes we did, thanks Gladys."

"Mm-hmm. An...?"

Clifford knows now is the time to set a limit. Otherwise the whole town will know every detail, if it already doesn't. "Gladys, Lily and I had a nice evening. And I'd like to keep some privacy in my life, if you don't mind."

"But aint you gonna at least tell your old Auntie what happened?"

"No."

There is a long silence. "I understand. Just want the best for you an Lily."

"Thank you, Gladys." Clifford could smell the wheels turning. Gladys wasn't much accustomed to being said no to, and she was almost certainly going to be working her other sources for intel, ASAP. "Well, Gladys, if that's all, I've got to go. Got a deadline to meet."

"Oh, course."

"I'll keep you posted what I learn from Angel."

"Thank you, nephew."

After lunch Clifford's back at the keyboard, but the words? They're somewhere other than his fingertips. Sitting there is futile. It's making him crazy, so he bundles up and heads for Angel's. The snow's let up some, but there's a good four, five inches on the ground. No plows have come through yet.

He drives past the grain elevator, all grey cement. White snow sticks to the windward sides of the silos. In places where the snow's melted, the cement's almost black. The plains, what's usually gold and blue are now white and grey. Vast expanses of white and grey, the world has lost its color. If not for ruts set in the snow, and the occasional roadside reflector, there'd be no telling where the road was. Everything is flat and featureless in the dim, diffuse light. Clifford makes a mental note to put his sleeping bag in the trunk and keep it there, just in case. It's easy enough to freeze to death out here.

Picking his way with care, Clifford sees a sign looming in the distance. As he gets closer, he's able to make out the details. "Angel Mahoney - Cartage," with a winged angel blowing a horn on top. The sign's made up from bent rebar welded together, now well rusted. There are sheds, and a house, and junk trucks scattered about in all directions, including the other side of the road as far as he can see. Windows are busted out, rust, bullet holes—there's not a truck that looks remotely roadworthy. He pulls his little Subaru into the yard, and points the nose out in case he needs to make a quick exit. After tooting the horn a couple times, three dogs come bounding out from one of the sheds. Their tails are not wagging. They leap at the car and growl and snap; it's all slobber, muzzles, and teeth up against the windows. Clifford is terrified.

He sits in the middle of all the snapping madness and decides to call Angel. The phone rings and rings as he's watching the house. There's no answer.

A ruddy-faced girl pokes her head out the door. She's scrawny and wears a dirty T-shirt six sizes too big, and her hair is matted. She calls to the dogs, but they don't listen. A man pokes his head out, yells at the dogs—to no effect—and then retreats. He comes back, hauls the girl into the house, and steps outside. He is filthy dirty. He has a handgun, points it to the sky, and quickly fires a few rounds. Clifford sees the tulip-shape flame burst from the muzzle, and he's thinking maybe it's best to get the hell out of here. But the dogs scatter, the man shoves the pistol into his pants, and walks toward Clifford. When he gets to the car, Clifford rolls down the window a couple inches.

"Goddamned dawgs! I pologize," says the man. "Im Angel, whor you?"

In as manly a tone as he can muster, Clifford identifies himself and adds, "I'm here for Gladys Calloway."

Angel, squirrely operator that he is, grins but doesn't look directly at Clifford. "Ol Gladys. Havent heard from her in a coyotes time. What all she up to?" Angel wraps his arms around himself and looks this way and that. He's shaking. "You wanna come inside? Dawgs wont bother you none."

"You sure?"

"Oh yeah, they all fine. Just dont touch em." Clifford, while not especially comforted, gets out of the car. The dogs run up and start sniffing him. "You got a dog at home?" asks Angel. Clifford shakes his head. "Good. Now, like I say, dont touch em." The dogs, their bodies taut and shaking, continue sniffing. Their hackles are up. "Just cmon with me. No never mind em." Clifford follows Angel along a narrow path winding through all the snow-covered junk. Inside the house, Clifford's nose is hit hard with a foul smell, a rancid combination of burned bacon fat and, what? Motor oil and grease. A big-screen TV in the corner flashes images of cars overturning and people getting blown up. Angel grabs a remote and mutes the sound, but the images continue. "Goddamn news," he says, "never anythin good. Dont know why I watch it. Have a seat." Angel points Clifford toward the sofa. It's covered with dog hair and ground-in dirt. Nonetheless, Clifford sits down and so does Angel. "What all Gladys be needin?" he asks.

Clifford notices three little children's faces peering at him around the corner. Haunted, silent little faces. Uncertain what to make of it all, he looks at Angel and says, "She's decided to move her nightclub and would like you to do the hauling."

"Easy enough. Where she movin to?"

"Just a different lot at Golden Gardens. Less than a mile."

"What she doin that for?"

"She's got a dispute with a neighbor at the current location."

"Path a least resistance," says Angel, his eyes darting to the big screen.

"That's about it," replies Clifford.

"Well you tell Gladys Im awful sorry to hear she goin through this. Gladys is a fine, fine woman. Heart a gold." Angel again looks at the TV. A ball of flame erupts under a Humvee, engulfs it, and the truck flips into the air. "*Damn*," says Angel under his breath. He turns to Clifford. "Now where was I? Uh, sure. When she gonna need haulin?"

"Probably the end of next week. You can do it?"

"Yep. Thatll give me time to get one a those shit heaps out there to run. An with luck, the snowll melt off."

"Is there a number where we can reach you?"

"Home phone."

Clifford nods. This is the number no one's ever answered. He places his hands on his knees. "Well, thank you, Angel. We'll be in touch and look forward to the end of next week." He stands up. He wants to leave this place, now.

"You bet. Give my greetins to Ol Gladys, wont you?"

"Will do," says Clifford as walks to the door. He waves to the children, who remain silent and do not wave back. "The dogs will be OK?"

"Oh yeah, they know ya now. Just dont touch em."

"Right," says Clifford. For him this will not be a problem. He shakes Angel's hand and takes his leave. The dogs follow him to his car, sniffing at him and growling. Clifford has the uneasy feeling the slightest misstep on his part and he's going to get bitten. Inching along he keeps his hands in his pockets. He slips into his car and slams the door. Safe at last. The dogs again erupt into barking and snapping, pink and black muzzles, yellow teeth, slobber and claws in all directions up against the car. Clifford starts the engine, puts it in gear and gasses it, hoping and praying he doesn't get stuck, hoping and praying the next time he calls Angel, the guy will just answer the phone.

At home after dinner, he calls Lily and tells her about his adventures.

Alarmed, she asks, "You didn't get bit? Are you OK?"

"No, no, I'm fine," says Clifford. "My car got scratched up, but it wasn't any showpiece to start with."

"That Angel Mahoney. I don't like him at all. His wife left him, left him with three children. The whole thing. Those poor little kids, and the conditions they call home. Nothing but trouble."

"No kidding. I hope he can actually get the job done for Gladys. There wasn't one truck he had that looked like it'd run. He said he'd get it together."

"Good luck on that. Did you have your pie for breakfast?"

"Mm… yes. Better with coffee than beer." Lily laughs and Clifford continues, "It was good. Not as good as your kisses." They talk as young sweethearts do, yearning for each other, already so full of the future.

Clifford looks at his watch. It's almost nine. "Lily, I told Gladys I'd give her a call, and I don't want to be too late."

"Well, sweet dreams then," says Lily.

Clifford melts. Sweet dreams… "Wow," he pauses, "you too, Lily." He thinks he's falling in love.

He calls Gladys. When she answers, right away Clifford picks up on the slur in her speech.

"Well howdy, Cliff," she says. "Howed your day go?"

"Good. I lined up Angel. More or less."

"Hope you didnt get bit."

"No. How'd you know?"

"I been out there a time or two. Dawgs he has, dont make no never mind which er when, they always been vicious." Gladys chuckles. "So dont take it personally."

"I'll remember that. How are you doing?"

"Oh hell, Im sittin here medicatin my demons. Im OK. Men got a lot done today, spite the snow. Tell me how it went with Angel. Hes a character, aint he?"

"To put it mildly. He said he'd have a 'shit heap,' I mean, a truck, running by next week and could do the job. I wouldn't hold my breath."

"Hell do it. I known Angel since he was a tadpole. He might not make the best first impression, but he does what he says. Any day thats bettern appearances in my book."

"You got a point."

"Listen Hon, Big Daddy just arrived. I gotta go. You an Lily gonna be seein any a each other soon?"

Clifford shakes his head, smiles, and decides he's going to leave it at, "We may."

"Well good. Cliff, I sure preciate your help."

"My pleasure, Gladys. You take care and say hi to Big Daddy for me."

"Will do."

Clifford hangs up, thinking he likes becoming part of the family.

.   .   .

Big Daddy comes in out of the cold, looking tired. He sees Gladys in her La-Z-Boy, their eyes meet, and they share a warm smile. "Glad to see my man," says Gladys. She attempts to get herself out of the chair.

"No need gettin up. Looks like youre doin well to take a load off," says Big Daddy. He walks over to Gladys, who has her arms out, leans over into her embrace, and gives her a kiss.

"Glad youre here, Honeybuns. Its been a day. Help yoursef if youre needin a libation."

"Yeah, let me see what all you got." Big Daddy peels off his coveralls, which are soaked and filthy, and drapes them over one of the dinette chairs. He goes into the kitchen.

"I heard from Sheriff Dalhart today," says Gladys.

Big Daddy pokes his head out of the kitchen. "Whatd he want?"

"Weaselbomb called and read him the riot act. That woman. She needs a man er somethin. Somethin to keep her occupied. Anyway, I told Chuck we was just doin maintenance, that we werent inside or nothin. He asked me what was this he heard bout a reopenin."

"Whatd you say?"

"I told him we was just gettin ready an left it at that. He was happy." Big Daddy has himself a beer in one hand and a bag of chips in the other, and he settles onto the sofa. "Howd it go for you all?" asks Gladys.

"We got most a Mommas unplugged. Course we have to get inside to split the two halves apart."

"Dont worry bout it, well just do it."

"An we got another problem."

"Like we need another. Whats that?"

"The wheels from the undersides is missin. You dont got em around anywhere?"

"Nope."

"Well, I checked, and theys a size different than most. But theres one trailer in the park with the same size."

"Shouldnt be a problem to borry em."

"No, shouldnt. Ceptin theys on Weaselbombs trailer."

Gladys snorts into her drink. "Well shit," she gasps and slaps her knee. Wouldnt you know it. Whater we gonna do?"

Big Daddy grins and there's a twinkle in his eye. "We gonna create a little diversion, somethin irresistible to Weaselbomb, an then we gonna help ourselves. She wont ever know the difference."

"Whats this 'little diversion' gonna be?"

"Dont know yet."

.   .   .

Clifford shows up at *The Trumpet* bright-eyed and bushy-tailed. He knows this is the day to do or die. His deadline is 5 p.m., and he doesn't have a single word written. The voicemail light on his phone is blinking, so he puts three sticky notes over it. Let it blink. Cathi's wiggling around, but she's leaving early for the weekend to go up to Wichita to be with her hubby. One less distraction, which is good. Clifford turns on his computer, sits back, and cracks his knuckles while it grinds away. When the machine finally comes to life, he starts to type.

The continued operation of Momma's Little Harry, a nightclub in the Golden Gardens retirement community 3 miles west of town on State Route 16, is uncertain. Spriggs County Sheriff Charles "Chuck" Dalhart has impounded the property based on ongoing complaints from neighbor Enid Witzle, who claims, "Theyre disturbin the peace...."

Founder, Owner, General Partner of Momma's, and longtime resident of Golden Gardens, Gladys Calloway, disputes this claim, "We aint done nothin wrong...."

A hearing on the matter in Spriggs County Court is set for the 5th of December 2011, time to be announced.

Momma's Little Harry is a topless bar, primarily serving the trailer park community. Founded six years ago, it is very popular with its customers. "The boys an me, we all love the place," says Golden Gardens resident Bill Dukish....

"So far, so good," thinks Clifford. He wonders if he should mention the encounter with Meow Meow. No, best to stick to what's relevant. He keeps pecking away.

.   .   .

Meanwhile, Gladys and Big Daddy are drinking coffee and strategizing. "Hower you gonna distract Weaselbomb?" asks Gladys.

"I been talkin to Sam an Bill an Old Brucey and theys gonna talk to George Carson an then theys gonna talk to their wives. Were proposin a little mornin tea over at Bills, bein as it is far away as possible from Mommas. The teas gonna be a hush-hush meetin just for womenfolk who supposedly want to close Mommas for good. An a course Weaselbombll be invited. When the tea gets started its gonna be all nice an social for a spell, an the tea, least Weaselbombs, is gonna be spiked. An spiked good! Ladiesll take it from there. Wish I could be there to see her face when she takes that first sip! Shell be welcome, shell be *encouraged*, to spend the day, the night, long as it takes. Be the day a the big move, so we got to cordnate with Angel."

Gladys gets right on the phone and calls Angel and gets no answer. "Damn," she says. "Wonder if that bandycoot ever gets it that answerin the phone an doin business might be related." She then calls Clifford. "Cliff, Honey, Angel aint answerin his phone."

"No surprise there," says Clifford.

"You be willin to head out there agin? For your Auntie Gladys?"

Clifford's not too keen on the idea but he agrees. "Can't make it today, got a deadline to meet, but tomorrow."

"Thatd be fine. I sure do preciate it."

Later in the day, Clifford calls Lily to talk about getting together over the weekend. He mentions, "Gladys asked me to go out to Angel's again tomorrow. I'm not even going to bother calling."

Lily turns into a protective she wolf on him. "I'm not going let you get bitten! I'll go out with you." The way she says it, Clifford knows this is not an option but a foregone conclusion.

"Well—"

"I'm going with you."

"Thank you, Lily," he says, knowing the path of no resistance is in reality his only option.

That afternoon, at 4:36 p.m. to be precise, Clifford hands his first installment of the story to Mr. Biotte, who is deep into the Sunday edition. A twister through his office might help organize things. He looks at Clifford over his glasses as the budding journalist hands in his first big story. He scans it and thinks for a moment. Clifford's beginning to squirm. Mr. Biotte looks up and smiles. "Been quite a week, hasn't it?"

"Yes, sir."

"Good work, Clifford. Have a good weekend."

"Thank you, sir. You too. Let me know if you need any changes."

"I will."

.　.　.

The next morning starts cold and crisp. The sky is a fathomless deep blue, and sunlight reflecting off the snow is enough to nearly blind a person. Clifford goes over to Lily's. She greets him at the door with a hug and a kiss. Clifford's getting used to the idea of hugs and kisses. Lily's ready to go, but she pauses outside the door. Before she locks it, she turns, runs in, and grabs a baseball bat which is leaning against the wicker rocker, and rushes back out.

This worries Clifford. He asks, "What's *that?*"

"It's my Louisville Slugger. I played Little League when I was a kid."

"But why are you bringing it?"

"I told you last night I wasn't going to let you get bit, and I meant it. One of those dogs gets too close, and he'll wish he hadn't."

Lily has her jaw set. Clifford asks, "What about Angel? He might be a little upset if you start clubbing one of his dogs." He looks at Lily with raised eyebrows. "You know he has a gun, and seems to make liberal use of it."

"Self-defense. Dogs don't know any better than to go after people, but for Angel to have them running around free? He should know better. I'll take my chances." Once in the car, Lily sits erect, she turns face forward, and stares out the windshield. Finally she asks, "Are we going to leave?"

Clearly, Lily has her mind set, and she means business. "Yeah," says Clifford, "let's get it over with." They get to Angel's and the yard is now a wallow of mud. No way is he driving in there, so he parks on the shoulder of the road and toots the horn. The dogs come bounding out, putting on the same show as last time, but they stop at the gate.

Lily's about to get out of the car when Clifford touches her arm. She glares at him. "Let's wait a moment," he says. The last time, Angel came out and brought them into line." This time, however, there's no Angel, and no children. Could be no one's home. Clifford calls, but the phone rings and rings. He's just about to give up when someone answers.

"What you want?" croaks the voice. It's Angel, talking as though he has a mouthful of crushed gravel. He's probably hung over.

"Hello, Angel, it's Clifford. I'm parked out front. I wanted to talk with you about hauling the doublewide for Gladys. She—"

"Yeah. Gimme a minute an Ill be out." Without further ado, Angel hangs up.

In a moment, Lily and Clifford can see him emerge from the hovel. The dogs quiet themselves and look back at their master. He's pulling up his pants and zipping the fly. "Disgusting," mutters Lily. He's got on just a filthy T-shirt. He stops, looks at the sky, rubs his face, and steps back inside. He comes out again wearing a winter jacket. He whistles at the dogs and they go to him. Clifford and Lily get out of the car. Lily is carrying the bat. "I'm not going to take any crap, just so you know," she growls.

"Just stay calm," says Clifford, not feeling at all calm himself. They make their way toward the house, and the dogs start running for them. Clifford's heart is pounding.

Angel hollers at them. "You goddamned sums a bitches! Get back here!" The dogs slow, stop, and turn their heads. They yearn for their quarry, but stay put while Lily and Clifford walk up to them. Lily raises the bat, and she's ready to swing. "Whos that you brung with you?" calls Angel.

"It's Lily Calloway!" Lily hollers back. The dogs, miraculously, just stand there and watch the two walk by.

"Well. Lil-y Call-o-way." Angel looks her up and down. Leering at her, he says, "My, my, how you grown up. Downright blossomed. *Mm-mh!*" Angel notices the bat. In mock consternation, he snickers and asks, "Now whats a pretty little thing like you gonna do with that bat. *Club* me?"

Clifford can feel his hackles rising.

"I more had in mind your dogs, Angel. They don't seem much of a problem this morning, but yeah, you too if you don't watch your step."

Angel looks at Clifford. "Cliff, we got us a wildcat here this mornin. *Real wildcat!*"

"Don't push it, Angel," says Lily, her chest rising and falling. She's ready to pounce.

"Cliff, you said this was a business call. Obviously, it aint social." Angel scratches himself. "What kin I do for you?"

Clifford positions himself between Lily and Angel. "Gladys'd like you to move the doublewide this coming Thursday. Think that'd work?"

"Yeah. Still havent figgered out whicha these pieces a shit will run. But yeah, Thursday otta work fine. You tell Miss Gladys Ill be there, ready to roll."

"Late morning?"

The dogs have snuck up behind Lily and are sniffing her. Angel stamps his foot to scare them off, but Lily, not realizing what's going on, lunges at Angel with the bat.

He cowers and yells, "Whoa! Lit-tle *Lay*-dee!" The dogs start barking and snapping.

Lily swings around with the bat and holds her ground. The dogs back off but keep barking.

Angel turns to Clifford. "Thursdayll be fine, late mornin. Meantime, I think you otta get this wildcat offa my property. Im askin kindly."

"I'll relay to Gladys you'll be there," says Clifford. "Thank you, Angel." He turns to Lily. "How about we get going?"

"Fine by me. *Fine* by me," sneers Lily. She and Clifford turn and slog their way through the mud to the car.

"Lookin nice, girlykins," calls Angel.

"Please, Lily, don't even look at him," says Clifford.

"*Real* nice!"

When they get into the car, Clifford takes a deep breath and says, "Lily, I've got to hand it to you, but please be careful."

Lily is fuming, and tears well in her eyes. "I'm not taking any shit from that, that, he gives *swine* a bad name!" Clifford reaches over and wipes the tears off her cheeks.

"And you shouldn't have to," he says. "I'm touched you're so looking out for me."

Lily smiles, pulls a tissue from her purse, wipes her eyes, and blows her nose. "I don't know what I'd do if anything happened to you."

.   .   .

The next week Gladys and her gang are right out straight. Faced with the problem of getting Big Daddy inside Momma's—he won't fit through the kitchen vent—she goes to the feed store to buy bolt cutters. Everybody at the store knows her, and she'd rather not get into conversation about what she's up to, so Gladys marches in, picks out the biggest pair they have, and goes straight to the cash register. Clyde, who's been there forever and is the biggest busybody in town, eyes them suspiciously. He picks them up to find the price tag.

"Whater you gonna do with these here bolt cutters, Gladys?" he asks.

"Cut bolts." Gladys knows the less said, the better.

With concerted effort, Clyde punches the keys of the old manual cash register. "With tax theyll be $57.83."

"For made in China, them aint cheap," says Gladys. She pulls three twenties from her purse and hands them over. "Shoots the hell outta those."

"Yep." Clyde counts out her change. "Thatll make ninety, fifty eight, and twoll make sixty. Thank you very much." He looks at her and grins.

"Thank you, Clyde," says Gladys.

"You're welcome. An Gladys, just so you know, thems wont cut the shackle of a padlock, but they will cut the hoop of the hasp." Clyde, still grinning, winks at her.

A little flustered, Gladys says, "Why thank you, Clyde, for the expert advice. Thats small-town service with a smile. I preciate it."

"Youre welcome."

"Hope we maybe see you out to Mommas real soon," she says.

Clyde is dying to ask questions, but thinks twice about it. "I spect you will," he says. "Thats the best news I had all day."

Late that night Gladys bundles up and heads over to Momma's with the bolt cutters. What she's doing is serious lawbreaking and she knows it. So it just wouldn't be fair to ask Big Daddy or anyone else to do it. She's got to go this one alone. The stars are out, and the weather's been holding, Gladys loves looking at the stars, all so far away, and all twinkly like they're saying hello. She picks out a bright one and makes a wish on it. She wishes for good weather and that all goes well, that nobody gets hurt.

Dry grasses crunch under her step as she approaches the trailer. Gladys is trying to be as quiet as she can. She doesn't want any dogs barking. All you need is one of them to start, and before you know it they all join in and people get to looking around. And that'd be sure trouble.

She makes it up the steps. So far, so good. The starlight is just enough that she can make out what she's doing. Twice she snips the hoop Sherriff Dalhart's lock is hanging from. She tries it and the lock slips through the cut. Pretty pleased with herself, she stands back and looks at her work. She's done as neat a job as possible. From the road you'd never know anything had happened. Tomorrow night, Big Daddy and the men will be able to get inside to do what's needed to split Momma into two.

Coming off the steps, Gladys drops the bolt cutters. They make a loud clang on the handrail. "Damn it!" she hisses, and sure enough one of the nearby little yippers sounds the alarm. Gladys knows she's got to make a run for it. She grabs the cutters and skedaddles. Before she's to the road, other dogs have joined in and she sees a front porch light come on. Just keep movin, ol girl, she thinks, just keep movin. Well, Gladys isn't as young as she used to be, and not quite as buff. Everything starts to hurt. Her body isn't liking this at all. A couple of folks call out to their dogs, "Buster, shut the hell up!" and "Now Skippy, get in here. Must be coyotes."

Yeah, must be coyotes, thinks Gladys. A big one, an the wyliest of the pack. She snickers as she scoots along.

When she gets back to her trailer, she sees lights on at Big Daddy's, so she decides to knock on the door.

"Who is it?" he calls in his serious man voice. She can hear him mutter, "What the hell at this hour?" The trailer shakes as he comes toward the door. Gladys knocks again. "Who the hell is it?"

"Me, Honeybuns," she coos.

Big Daddy opens the door. "You OK?"

"Yeah. I come by for a little visit."

Big Daddy's face lights up. "Well, you come on in then. Dont delay!"

Gladys steps inside, sets the bolt cutters on the coffee table, and turns to give Big Daddy a kiss. But he's looking at the tool, puzzled, "What in hell you doin with those?"

Gladys can't resist. "I was just thinkin you needed a little calmin down." She pantomimes operating the cutters and says, "snip, snip."

Alarmed, Big Daddy replies, "But Honeybunch, then thered be no more visitin."

Gladys thinks about this. "You got a point." She gives him a kiss. "Never mind then. How long a woman got to be around this joint before she gets a drink?"

"Come right this way, little lady." Big Daddy leads Gladys into the kitchen. "What all you like?"

"Hot tea an a brandy would hit the spot. Keep me up and get me down."

"Im likin the sounds a that." Big Daddy tends to Gladys' refreshment as she fills him in on her hoop-cutting escapades. "All these years," he says, grinning, "I didnt know you was such a lawbreaker."

"Im a woman a many talents," says Gladys. She swivels her hips.

"That you are. An I like em all." Big Daddy puts his arms around Gladys, kisses her, and rubs her back. She coos and sighs, puts her arms around her man, and holds him tight.

"An I like all a them man talents you got. Thats what Im here for."

.   .   .

The next night, as soon as it's dark, Big Daddy, Sam, and Bill sneak into Momma's. They light the candles they've brought and set them here and there around the trailer. Like three bears dancing by the flickering light, they pry and unscrew and cut the doublewide in two. By the time they get to the last few nails, the halves creak and snap and lurch apart on their own, more than they'd counted on. Big Daddy stands there astride the two and watches anxiously as the gap in the roof widens. "Hope she dont just keep a goin," he says. Sam and Bill look on, and when the trailer stabilizes they clap and hoot. Through the roof they can see the inky blue black sky and all those stars.

"Put a little poly over it an itd be kinda like a skylight," says Bill, matter-of-factly.

"Maybe if we cant get her sealed up at the new location," says Big Daddy. "I think we best not dilly dick around. Lets get outta here, but no quick moves!" They blow out the candles and the three bears tippy-toe to the front door lightly as mice. Big Daddy pauses by the door to fiddle with the latch, and the trailer lurches under their collective weight. "Hurry up! Lets git goin!" Once outside, he puts the lock back in the hasp. "Were good. Just hope the wind dont pick up, or it snows. That could be trouble."

.   .   .

Wednesday morning Gladys is sipping coffee at the table in the breakfast nook in her bathrobe and slippers. The fan in the gas heater buzzes, which used to annoy the hell out of her, but now she's got other things on her mind. The table is covered with to-do lists. She looks at them and wonders, will it all get done? The phone rings. She doesn't want to answer it but knows she better.

"Gladys, this heres Angel. I got some bad news."

"Boy, you aint only begun to have bad news if youre callin to cancel on me."

"Well, I aint cancelin, but I got to postpone."

"Thats as bad as cancelin, Angel."

"I was afraid a that."

Gladys' pulse has already jumped a notch. "What alls the problem?"

108

"Caint get the truck to run. It used to."

Gladys shakes her head. If this boy had half a brain to work with, he'd really be dangerous. "Angel, they all used to run at some point."

There's a pause and then he says, "Yeah, I guess youre right."

"Please do whatever you can to get it to run. I got a lot restin on movin Mommas tomorrow. Not to mention looks like the weathers turnin agin."

"I understand. Ill do my best."

"Thank you, Angel. Keep me posted." As Gladys hangs up the phone, she decides she better pay Angel a little visit. A few little words of encouragement can't do any harm. She knows from past experience Angel isn't the brightest bulb in the package. Damn truck probably doesn't even have gas in it. Be just like Angel to not even think to check.

Gladys gets herself dressed. It doesn't take much to make oneself presentable enough to visit Angel. At the last minute before stepping out the door, she grabs her work boots and insulated coveralls. They might come in handy.

The old Toronado doesn't especially want to start, but Gladys coaxes it to life. It sputters and backfires as she chugs out of the trailer park, leaving a trail of oily smoke in its wake. Once on the open road and warmed up, though, the car cruises along. The ol girl runs pretty good when you let her build up a head a steam, thinks Gladys, kinda like me. It glides over the bumps. Gladys loves that big car ride, like floating on a cloud. The Toronado is the modern-day prairie schooner, and she's the captain of the ship. Nice to get out and about, and a relief to get away from all her cares for a few moments.

She cruises through town. There's Clifford's car outside *The Trumpet*, there's Lily's car outside Dr. McNulty's office. So the two youngins are busy at work. It makes Gladys happy to know she played a small part in these two being lovebirds. Young love's the sweetest, fresh and new, not yet trampled on by life.

Trucks are coming and going around the grain elevators, and beyond there's Dickie's QuickGo and the motel, and then she's out of town and on the prairie. She's reminded this is the way she used to drive to the turkey plant every day. A problem with staying in one place for so long is you're never far from the past. That whole chapter of her life, losing her boy. Memories of it only bring her sadness. There was a time she couldn't stand to drive out here. Now it's just a twinge, but it's a sharp one.

Angel's place appears out in the distance. Makes a pigsty look like a swanky joint, thinks Gladys. Really a shame, some people live worse than animals. Eyeing the yard and the ruts in the mud, she decides to park on the side of the road. She can see Angel's butt and legs sticking out from under the hood of his old Mack dual axle. Used to be a farm truck until Angel converted it into a towing rig. If the poor old thing could talk, thinks Gladys, but then again, maybe better it can't. She knows where this will go, so she puts on her work boots, gets out of the car, and then pulls on the coveralls and zips them up so they're snug. When she slams the car door, the dogs sound the alarm and come running at her ready to attack. But haul up short when they recognize Gladys. They wag their tails and loiter around as if to apologize for the ruckus. "You all just a bunch a bull shitters," says Gladys. "I wonder where you learnt that from."

She sneaks up on Angel and shouts, "Hey there you scallywag! I come here for the good news." The dogs swarm and snuffle around her.

Startled, Angel jerks his head up and hits it with a dull thud on the underside of the hood. "Damn! Ugh, that hurt."

Then he then drops the wrench he was using. Gladys hears it pling and clunk its way deep into the bowels of the engine bay. "Aw, *shit!*" hisses Angel. He turns and peers out, sees Gladys, and grins. "Gladys!" he says. "You really shouldnt sneak up on a feller like that. How the hell are ya?"

"Im fine, Angel," she replies. "Finer if you can get this truck goin."

Angel hops down, pushes the hair out of his eyes, and then wipes his grease-covered hands on his overalls. "I dont know whats wrong with it. She cranks an farts, but she dont run."

"Got gas in it?"

Angel raises his eyebrows like he hadn't thought of this one. He smirks and shrugs his shoulders. "I think so."

Gladys isn't the least bit surprised but still she can't believe it. She wonders if one of Angel's kids ties his shoes for him. "You think so," she says, "but you dont know so." She grins at him, and shakes her head. "Do you spect we otta check?"

They go over to the tank hanging below the driver's door. Angel spins the metal cap off, sticks his nose in the filler, and takes a good whiff. "Whoa!" He stumbles back with a nose full of fumes. "Smells like it!" In the meantime Gladys finds a long twig among the scrub growth, and strips off the bramble and branches. "Whater you gonna do with that?" asks Angel.

"Use it as a dipstick, you dipstick." She waggles it toward Angel for him to step out of her way, and he complies. She dips the twig in the tank so it taps the bottom and pulls it out. Four or five inches from the end are wet.

"Whered you learn that?" asks Angel.

"The college a hard knocks. Straight A student," Gladys replies. "You say she turns over?"

"Yes, maam, just barely." Angel's looking a little perplexed. "I din know you went to college."

Gladys just looks at him. "An she farts?"

"Yes, maam."

Gladys thinks on this for a moment, steps up on the front tire, and pokes her head under the hood. It smells strongly of gasoline. It's a mess under there, wires and tubing going in all directions, oil leaks caked with dirt, duct tape holding things together, and the remains of packrat nests stuffed in all the corners. She peers out at Angel, who's standing there with the blankest expression she's ever seen - excepting maybe on a cadaver. Wouldnt be hard to figger out whats goin on in that boys mind, thinks Gladys, cause theres so little of it. "You check the air cleaner?" she asks.

"No, maam."

"You got a screwdriver?"

"Yes, maam." Angel digs in his pocket and pulls out the grimy, well-hammered remains of a screwdriver. He hands it to Gladys.

She uses it to pry the clips off the big metal can that holds the air cleaner. Soon as the cover comes loose, packrat middens spill out. "I think this heres your problem," she says. "The ol girls nose is stuffed up." She peers into the filter, and three pairs of black beady eyes stare back at her. "Well looky, looky, we got us a nice little family livin in here!" She turns to Angel. "You got a good stout stick?"

"Lemme see what I kin come up with." Angel wanders off. Gladys watches him as he burrows into his own midden pile. Worn out broken junk and brightly colored children's toys all busted up are strewn in all directions. She hops down to look for a stick on her own. She knows there's a good chance Angel will forget what he's looking for and never come back.

Gladys finds a crowbar laying in the weeds. She picks it up, a perfectly good crowbar, all rusted, just lying there. She wipes away clods of mud, decides it ought to do the job, climbs back up under the hood of the truck, and pokes at the packrats. The more she pokes, the deeper they burrow in. "I spose if I had a brain the size of a goddamned raisin, Id do the same thing," she mutters to herself. She hits the far end of the can with the crowbar, and this prompts the packrats to get out. She keeps rapping on the can and finally they make a jump for it and scurry away.

Angel walks up with another slightly longer screwdriver. "Think thisll work?" he asks.

Gladys doesn't have the heart to tell him what she really thinks, so she says, "Itll help," and she takes it from him. She pokes and pries and coaxes the filter from the can. It's stuffed tight as a jar of dill pickles with little bits and pieces of packrat nest, and a lot of black pill-size poop. What a mess! She pulls the filter out and throws it on the ground. A big cloud of dust plumes from it and blows right back at them in the wind. "Damnit all!" she sputters and coughs. After cleaning the filter as best they can, and the housing, Gladys puts it all back together, eases herself down from the truck, and says, "Giver another one, Angel. This time put your foot on the floor an keep it there til I say to move it."

Angel climbs into the cab, does what he's been told, and turns the key. The engine turns over, *rawr, rawr, rawr… rawr…ra…* When it's just about to die, it farts. *Rawr… rawr…* and this time it catches. The engine bursts into mad life, sputters, backfires, stalls, and picks up again. Giant billowing clouds of black smoke come from the exhaust. Angel keeps his foot on the gas and the engine races, and then Gladys gestures for him to let off on it. The engine settles to a rough idle and farts a bit but keeps running. Angel hops down from the cab. He dances around in a little circle, hoots, and claps his hands. "Gladys you sure are somthin! You are a miracle!"

She winks at him. "Ill send you my bill. Just dont forget to fill up that tank when youre comin through town tomorrow mornin." She slaps Angel on the back.

"I wont. Ill be sure to," says Angel. "Im mighty obliged."

"I got miles to go fore I sleep," says Gladys. "We be seein you tomorrow."

"You bet."

Gladys looks at the sky and thinks no, she wouldn't bet. "An by the way," she says, "that werent too kind a way you treated my niece Lily the other day."

Angel looks at her wide-eyed. "She come on my property with a baseball bat threatenin to beat my dawgs."

"Cant say as I blame her. No excuse, Angel."

"Yes, maam."

Gladys walks out to the Toronado. Her back's already hurting from so much bending under the hood of that old truck. Clouds are getting thicker and the wind's out of the south, it's moisture coming in off the Gulf.

.   .   .

Back at Golden Gardens, a certain few of the upstanding community ladies are planning a little tea party, and Enid Witzle is invited. The gathering will be at Betty Carson's (George has elected to be elsewhere), and she's laid in a good supply of eggnog, extra tea bags, and a big bottle of dark rum. She also has the guest room fixed up. The other ladies will be bringing sweet treats and sandwiches. It's going to be a lovely time.

114

Big Daddy has been assembling his tool kit, everything he can think they might possibly need for the move. Jacks, come-along, lengths of chain, lug wrench, his portable compressor, blocking, hand tools. Extension cords. Shovels, pickax, peaveys. And a level for when they get to the new site. *If* they get to the new site. His jeep is stuffed to the gills.

Gladys has been mostly fretting. Pacing, worrying, checking her lists. Drinking too much coffee and bugging Big Daddy. Hoping and praying. Looking at the picture of her little Harry calms her.

.　.　.

First thing the morning of the big day, Lily and Clifford show up. They both have that happy faraway look that says maybe they didn't get a lot of sleep last night. They lug in grocery bags loaded with extra ground coffee and boxes of donuts to get the crew going, more coffee and sandwich fixings to feed the crew lunch, and more sandwich fixings and beer for the crew to celebrate with when the job is done.

Gladys winks at Lily. "Looks like maybe you didnt get much sleep, girl."

Lily blushes and smiles primly. "Got as much as I need, Auntie."

"Nice to see you two so happy," says Gladys.

"Thank you, Auntie. Would you help us put things in the fridge? We don't want to upset the applecart."

.　.　.

Old Brucey is positioned in Weaselbomb's neighborhood to keep an eye on her. He's out walking his dog (which he fondly refers to as the bottlebrush), and taking his time of it. This is not a problem. That little dog can sniff a single blade of grass for an eternity. Gladys asked Old Brucey about this once, how he managed to put up with it. Old Brucey smiled and said, "He loves the smells." The man loves his dog so, it nearly broke Gladys' heart. When he sees Weaselbomb leaving her trailer, he's going to call Gladys. Then, when Weaselbomb crosses the threshold into Betty's place, when the ladies actually have her in their grips, Betty's going to call Gladys.

The men arrive at Gladys', just as Clifford and Lily are laying out coffee and donuts. They're all a bit groggy but in good cheer. Big Daddy might be a smidge worried, but he hides it as best he can. When they get the call from Betty they'll spring, such as they're able, into action.

The phone rings and Gladys picks it up. "Brucey here. The bird is taking flight."

"Brucey, could you just give it to me in plain English?" snaps Gladys. She's a little on edge.

"Poetry is in my blood," he says, "but if I must, Weaselbomb has left her trailer."

"Thank you, Brucey. Why dont you an your hound hang for another minute or two. Case anythin changes, let me know. But then come on over to warm up and have some coffee and donuts."

"It would be my pleasure," says the old Hungarian.

Minutes pass. Gladys paces the floor. "Honeybunch, just relax," says Big Daddy smooth as butter. "Everthins gonna be OK."

Gladys stares at the floor. She doesn't look up. "I cant right now." The men give her space, but when they catch her eye they smile, trying to offer what little comfort they can. In a few minutes there's a knock at the door. Gladys jumps.

Lily answers it. It's Old Brucey and the bottlebrush. "Do come in," she says. "Get warmed up, we got coffee." Brucey

116

climbs in and lets the dog off the lead. The scrawny little thing immediately starts sniffing around the place.

"Amazin how that dog sniffs," says Gladys, hoping that he's not going to start marking his territory.

Brucey is peeling off his heavy overcoat. "He's happiest with his smells."

There's no call from Betty. No call, no call... "Whatin the hell could be goin on?" asks Gladys. She's beside herself with anxiety. "Maybe shes turned—"

The phone rings. Gladys lunges across the room to grab it.

"Gladys, this is Betty." She's speaking in a hushed tone. "Enids here and were gettin her settled in real nice like. Youre all clear."

"Thank you, Betty! Thank the Gawd amighty!" Gladys' eyes well with tears. "Please, you keep us posted if anythin changes."

"I will, Gladys. You have a nice day."

Gladys hangs up the phone, and Lily gives her a hug and says, "Everything's going to turn out fine, Auntie."

Gladys looks at Big Daddy and the men. "Bless your hearts. Its time to get a movin."

Big Daddy gives her a kiss. "Cmon fellers, lets get this thing done."

In the meantime over at Betty's, the ladies are all a twitter putting out sandwiches and treats and starting with a lovely cup of eggnog. Of course Enid's is special. She takes a sip and her eyes go wide. She glances at the other ladies, who give no sign anything is amiss. Enid smiles. "My, this is some eggnog," she croaks.

"Its the way we like it when we get together," replies Betty. The ladies nod in agreement. For a second, Betty feels bad for pulling this trick on Enid, but she doesn't feel bad enough. She's looking forward to having Momma's open again. It'll get George out from under her skirts once in a while. She holds a platter out to Enid, nicely arranged with delectables. "Please, have one," she says. "An ladies, lets have a little catch-up before we get down to *business*." She gives Enid a wink.

When they finish their first cup of eggnog, they move right to the second. "I... ruther... LIKE thish bevgerage. Oh! Silly me, I mean *eggrog*," says Enid, holding up her cup and waving it around for a refill.

"We also have tea," suggests Betty.

"No! Naw for me. I LIKE the *eggrog!*"

Betty thinks to herself, well, what the hell, looks like shes enjoyin herself. She freshens Enid's cup, helps herself to another mini eclair, and the ladies talk about news items of mutual interest.

Meanwhile, Big Daddy, Bill, Sam, and Clifford are at Weaselbomb's, peeling back the skirting and fixing to remove the wheels and tires from the trailer. It's up on jack stands, so she'll never know, unless of course the day comes she decides to move it. There's just four wheels on this model, so they'll be able to move only half of Momma's at a time. But of course all the tires are flatter than Kansas. Big Daddy's pleased with himself that he thought of this already and has his compressor on hand. They crawl around and strain and grunt like men do. The lug nuts are well rusted on. Big Daddy gets a length of iron pipe from the Jeep to put over the end of the wrench. Give him a lever long enough and there isn't a nut he can't bust free. No siree.

Big Daddy strains, the pipe bends, the other men move out of the way, and *creak! Gronk!* A little puff of rust pops from the nut, and ever so slowly it turns. "Thats the way we like em," says Big Daddy. They keep at it and in short order have all four wheels off. They put back the skirting, real careful like, and stand back and admire their work. "Never know nothin was touched," says Big Daddy. "Cmon boys."

They roll the four lumpy old tires over to Momma's and keep working. No time for dilly dickin around today.

. . .

Enid's drained her second cup and is turning into the life of the party. Waving the cup in the air, she hollers, "Nuther rground! On the mouse! Cmon girls!"

Betty has never seen Enid have such a good time. This might be turning a new leaf for her. "Sure you wouldnt like to switch to tea?" she asks.

"No! *Reggrog for me!* For ever bloody!" Enid laughs until she's gasping for air.

The ladies laugh with her. Betty holds up the bottle of rum and motions to them if they'd like to join in. All of them nod. What the heck, they're all starting to feel left out, so might as well join the fun!

"Was we gonta rawk about Mommas *Liddle you know Whut?*" asks Enid. The ladies fall silent. Enid looks around at them, pie-eyed. Betty swallows. "Naw!" continues Enid. "You know girls, *I had nuff a tit! I jus rutha peep mavin some... FUN!*" Enid starts to blubber, "*I neber* have so muk fun." She perks up. "Dringk uph, girls!"

. . .

Big Daddy and the boys have three of the four wheels on the first half of Momma's when they hear Angel approaching. He's still a mile away, but the old Mack announces itself, bellowing and grinding along, sounding like it's on a slippery slope toward the grave.

119

Angel arrives and leaves the truck running. He's smart enough to know some one of these times he shuts it down is gonna be its last. He walks up to where the men are grunting around tire number four, and pauses to stub a toe into the dirt. "You all er doin pretty good for a bunch a old buzzards!" he hollers. The dirt's feeling pretty soft. He notes to himself it could be a problem.

Clifford looks at Angel and hopes some day there might be something about this guy he'll find likeable. Some day.

"Mornin, Angel," says Big Daddy. "Fine day for a move, dontcha think?"

Angel looks at the sky. Clouds are still hangin to the south. "Long as they stay there, itll be fine nuff. Looks like you fellers almost ready. How bout I get the rig backed in?"

Big Daddy looks up at Angel and nods as he tightens down the last of the lug nuts. Bill, Sam, and Clifford go around and release the jack stands. Half of Momma's is ready to go. As Angel backs the truck in, Clifford notes the tires are sinking into the dirt. Not a whole lot, but enough to notice. Snowmelt from that last storm is not going to do them any favors.

.   .   .

Over toward Betty and George's place, you can hear the carrying on from three trailers away.

.   .   .

With Momma's hitched up to the old Mack, Angel climbs into the cab, puts her in double low range, and gives a tug. The truck bucks and shudders, but the wheels just spin. The trailer doesn't budge. "Might be the hubs is frozen," hollers Big Daddy. Angel tries nudging it in reverse. Nothing. But suddenly, creaking like an old ship, the trailer moves. Just a little bit. Angel pulls forward again. The truck is laboring for all she's worth. The tires sink and spin, but she gains a bit of momentum. And slowly, slowly, plowing deep ruts all the way, they make it to the road. Everybody's hooting with excitement.

Angel keeps moving. The men jump in the Jeep to follow.

Gladys, who's decided it's best to stay in her trailer, hears them coming. She's been pacing and talking to Harry's photo on the wall and getting in Lily's way as she's trying to prepare lunch. When Gladys hears the roar of the Mack, she runs outside. She jumps up and down, and cheers. A tower of black smoke rises from the truck's exhaust. The old beast is working hard. Lily comes out and puts her arms around Gladys. Angel gives them a thumbs-up from the cab, but he doesn't dare look at Lily.

Big Daddy gases the Jeep and passes Angel. He wants to get there first to direct him in. Angel comes in behind and grinds to a stop. He hops down from the truck and they congratulate each other and shake hands all around. Big Daddy has the corners of the site staked, and scopes it out with Angel. This is Angel's moment to shine. He does know how to maneuver a big rig, and he backs it in without a glitch.

With the first half of Momma's in position, the men scurry around, jack the corners, and pull off the wheels. Big Daddy looks at his watch. It's a little after noon. "Ladiesll be caterin lunch. Theyll bring it wherever we are. Lets keep on a roll." They throw the wheels on the bed of the truck and head back. By the time Gladys and Lily arrive with coffee and sandwiches, they have the wheels on her second half and the truck hooked up. It's pretty much ready to go.

While they're taking a break, slowly, silently, the old Mack sinks into the damp earth. As Angel finishes his second bologna and cheese sandwich, he happens to turn and look at the truck. "Oh holy shit!" he exclaims, standing there and gawking at it. The truck's sunk halfway up to the axles in the mud. He turns to the gathered crowd. "Whater we gonna do?"

"Maybe itll come free," says Big Daddy. "Give it a try."

"Im not likin this one bit," says Angel. He sucks his teeth as he climbs into the cab. When he gives the rig a nudge in low range, the tires spin and it sinks in more, nearly up to the axles. He shakes his head, curses, and punches the dashboard. He looks out the window at five forlorn faces.

"What are we gonna do?" Gladys asks Big Daddy.

"Lemme think on it." Big Daddy takes a little walk to the far end of the rig and stops and stands there for a minute. He looks at the prairie, how he loves this place. He turns around and comes back. "This is what we gonna do." He motions for Angel to get down from the cab.

"Angel, you stay here an stand guard. Everbody else, we all gonna fan out in the park, an wherever you see a truck or a Jeep or whatever. A *ridin lawnmower.* You knock on ever door. Ask em to come on over an bring their rig an a length a chain or come-along or whatever they got. We gonna have us a little tug a war. All a us against this mud." He stubs a clod with his toe. "An we gonna win. We gots to win."

.   .   .

Enid says to Betty, "Ish been ah loverly time. You stink I migh taksh a lil... sluteye for I... g..." Whether Enid nods off or passes out is not quite clear, but the ladies look at one another and agree they'll get her nice and comfy in the guest room, and then get back to the party.

.   .   .

122

Within a half hour, six men driving four by fours and two on riding mowers show up at the scene of Momma's stuck half. These guys are strutting what's left of their stuff and chomping at the bit to pull this old molar out. They know they can do it. These men have been dying for a mission, wanting to step out of their trailer homes with a sense of purpose. This is their time to show what they got, before it's too late.

Big Daddy rounds them up and shouts orders. "Short chains, long ones, well figger it out. Use low range if you got it," he barks. "Same for lockin diffs. Ridin mowers in the front—dont stop pullin til the trailers clear on the road."

The men all jump into action. Gladys stands by with Lily. She's never seen anything like it. She's feeling mighty loved, and a tightness in her throat. These old geezers, all of them, they're the ones who sit around Momma's, wink at the girls, make wise comments every now and then, and laugh and have some fun. And she and the girls and everybody takes it in stride. It's what they do. But having them show up like this? They aren't going to take no for an answer. God bless 'em.

They all hook up to the front of the Mack. Clifford stands out front to give the signal. Big Daddy scurries around to check that everything's secure. He gives Clifford the thumbs up and Clifford gives the OK.

This unleashes the wildest, most God-awful display of horsepower and grunt, willpower and determination. Engines roar and snarl, exhausts bark. Chains creak. Mud gets slung high into the air. Six pickup trucks, two lawnmowers, and one old Mack give their all. They strain and slither, they pull. And slowly, almost imperceptibly, Momma's begins to move.

The boys are screaming, hooting, shaking their fists out windows. Go! Go! Go! Men, don't let off. Clifford's waving his arms. C'mon! Put the hammer down and keep it down, this is it.

123

We got to do it. And Momma's rolls. The wheels sink in deep, but they pull hard. And she's on the road! Clifford swipes his hand across his neck. Cut it! But these men, together, they are going to see it through, all the way. It's a parade of manhood, a spectacle. A day that's going in the Panhandle history books. The day they all towed Momma's second half.

. . .

Enid stirs in bed. What is it she's hearing? She sits up, but she doesn't feel so good. Everything tilts in all directions. Wobbly, she gets up, she needs to use the ladies room.

. . .

The gang of straining vehicles comes to a stop at the new site. The men jump from their trucks and hug one another. Gladys hugs them. She's happier than she's been in years. They're dancing around, congratulating one another, back slapping and recounting tense moments.

The men decide to stick around, curious to watch Angel perform his backing up magic, and be there just in case. They glow in what it feels like to be needed, to be vital again. After they unhitch all the chains, Angel tucks the second half of Momma's right up next to the first. He hops out of the Mack, eyes the structures, and declares, "Looks like they grew there!"

Gazing upon the trailer halves on the new lot, Gladys can hardly believe it. She stands among the men, soaking in the goodness. "You fellers all have a open tab at the Grand Reopenin of Mommas. At her *new location*."

"Youaller... bunker abrest!" shouts a slurred, squeaky voice.

Gladys spins around. It's Weaselbomb. The poor thing is barely able to stand up, but she's wildly waving her arms in the air.

"Im baking a cigtizens awrest!"

Gladys' inclination is to light into her, but what would be the use? She wishes somehow or other she had a "go away" button to push, because if she did, right now, she'd push it for all it was worth.

The men are looking dumbfounded.

Betty Carson and the ladies come running, such as they can, and looking distraught. Panting, Betty says, "She snuck out on us. We came after her soon as we knew!"

Seeing she's getting nowhere, Weaselbomb squeaks, "Im ralling sha Theriff!" She turns on the ladies and hisses at them, "Dirty trick pew layed on me!" She stalks and stumbles away, punching the air haphazardly with her tiny fists.

"And we were havin such a nice time!" says Betty.

"Betty, girls," says Gladys, "you all done good. There aint a whole hell of a lot Weaselbomb or anybody can do about us now." She sweeps a hand in the direction of Momma's, such as it is. "Looky! We done the deed!"

The ladies break into polite applause. Big Daddy clears his throat.

"Yes, Honeybuns?" asks Gladys.

"Just the same, I think it might be a good ideer if we all, an Angel, an you ladies, if you clear out. Sheriff might show up, an the fewer there is around to get in trouble, the less trouble therell be."

"Good thinkin," says Gladys. She turns to Angel as the crowd starts to disperse. "How bout you an me settle up?"

Angel looks at Gladys and grins. "How bout you jus pay for my fuel? Rest dont worry bout."

"Oh, Angel—"

"It was you fixed my truck. Remember?"

"OK. Fuel. An beer?"

"Deal. Fifty dollarsll cover it."

Gladys reaches inside her brassiere, pulls out a roll of cash, and peels a fifty out of the middle. She hands it to Angel.

"Thank you, maam."

"Thank you, Angel, fer all you done. Couldnt a done it without you."

Before Angel can get in the Mack, they hear the siren and then they see the red flash of the bubblegum machine peek over the horizon. "Shit," says Angel. "I cant stand nuther mistermeaner. Got too many as it is!"

But before he can get the truck moving, in a spray of gravel Sheriff Dalhart wheels up in the cruiser. He shuts off the siren but leaves the beacon going, for effect. He gets out, puffs himself up, and puts on his hat. He's looking like a confused mix of not too pleased and dying to laugh his head off. His heavy leather patrol belt creaks as he walks. He approaches the motley little group.

The sheriff tips his hat to Gladys and Lily. "Afternoon, ladies," he says. "I got a complaint bout a—" he checks his notepad, "— maybe looks like a traffic violation."

"Gawd damnf it Wheriff! Arrist em tall! Gawd damn it!" It's Weaselbomb, frothing at the bit.

The sheriff turns and stands his ground. Inside, secretly, he's scared as hell of this little banshee. Slowly he places his hand on his sidearm, hoping she notices the gesture. Weaselbomb keeps coming. "Enid, stop right there," he says. He tips his head and gives her a steely stare. Enid stops and catches her breath. She gulps. "Enid, Im gonna give you all a chance to turn tail an go home. Right now. If you dont, I will place you under arrest

126

for assaultin an officer, public drunkenness, and disturbin the peace. Have I made myself clear?"

"But… But!"

"Enid—"

"Towin pithout a wermit! Other law brea—"

"Now, Enid." The sheriff points his finger in the general direction of her trailer home and says, "Go home."

Enid swallows hard and pouts, but she's gotten the hint. She turns. "Gawd damn it all to, all to…" she sputters to herself as she skittles and weaves down the road.

The sheriff turns back to business. He looks at Angel. "Whater you doin here?"

"Leavin."

"Good. I suggest you continue with what you was doin."

"Yessir. Thank you, sheriff." Everybody steps out of the way, Angel climbs into the truck, salutes the sheriff, puts it in gear, and gets her rolling. Grinning, he gives the horn two good blasts, which makes everybody jump. He chugs away in a billowing cloud of black smoke.

"Sheriff, I believe this is your property." Gladys hands him the padlock. "No harm done to it, but I do owe you a hasp."

Sheriff Dalhart takes the padlock. "Thank you, Gladys." He looks at it, ponders it. He's trying to figure out what he's going to say next and clears his throat. "That hasp, Gladys, was Spriggs County property. Breakin it was breakin the law. Is that clear?"

"Yessir," gulps Gladys. Her knees are suddenly feeling a bit shaky.

"This is your first offense," says the sheriff very sternly. "As such Im gonna give you a warnin." The sheriff creaks back to his cruiser and gets his official aluminum clipboard with the standard all-purpose carbonless triplicate warning and citation forms and starts filling one out. He's frowning. They taught him to always frown when filling out one of these forms. He looks at his watch and continues to write. Inside, he's about to bust his gut. "This warnin states that you are to deliver a new hasp to my office within twenty-four hours. If you fail to do so, I will bring the full weight of the laws at my disposal down upon you. Kinda like locusts. Is that clear?"

"Yessir."

"Furthermore, if I ever catch you breakin Spriggs County property again—" he barely catches himself starting to snicker, "—it will be a citation. Not a warning. Is that clear?"

"Yessir."

He hands the clipboard and his pen to Gladys. He points to the box next to the X he just wrote, and says, "Sign here."

Gladys signs the form and hands back the clipboard. Sheriff Dalhart pulls out the pink copy and hands it to Gladys. "Have a nice day." he says.

"Thank you, Chuck," says Gladys. "You too."

He turns to leave, stops, and turns to Gladys again. "Id like my pen back."

Gladys looks at the pen, smirks, and hands it to him. "Its a nice one," she says.

The sheriff simply nods, turns, and stalks back to the cruiser. He gets in and slowly drives out of the park. The tires crunch on the gravel in that special slow-rolling cop-car way. When he gets to the highway he turns on the siren and floors it, just for the fun of it. And he howls and laughs himself all the way back to town. That Gladys! Dumb as a fox! Moving Momma's the way she did, bless her heart. He makes a mental note to be at the grand reopening for sure. It's going to be a hell of a good time.

With all the excitement over, Gladys and her gang and Old Brucey's little bottlebrush go back to Gladys' trailer to celebrate. Lily and Clifford make sandwiches until they run out of fixings while Gladys keeps the beers coming. They have themselves a hoot, recounting the adventure, the close calls, the moments they thought they were a goner, and ultimately their success.

.   .   .

Next morning, after Gladys and Big Daddy have coffee and good-bye kisses, Gladys' first order of business is to go to town to the feed store. Clyde, as usual, is behind the counter.

"Mornin, Gladys," he says.

"Mornin, Clyde. Youre lookin pretty perky this mornin."

"Always am, Gladys. Just lovin life. What can we do for ya?"

"You sell hasps?"

Clyde smiles and practically skips out from behind the counter. "Right this way."

"I dont know what youre takin," says Gladys, "but I want some."

Clyde turns as they're walking down an aisle and whispers. "No shortage a lovin, Gladys, if you know what I mean." He winks and adds, "Thats my secret."

"Good for you, Clyde! More people get a little regular lovin and not get all het up about it, the world be a happier place."

"Gladys, I couldnt agree with you more," says Clyde.

They get to the hasp display. Clyde reaches into a paperboard box, pulls one out that's heavy galvanized steel, and hands it to Gladys. "This is same as what the county buys."

"Zactly what I'm lookin for."

"Just one?"

"Yep, thatll doer."

With hasp in hand, Gladys marches over to the county office building. The little town is near as dead as a town can be. Crossing Main Street, she stops in the middle and looks both ways. Nothing. Not a car, far as Kansas one way, New Mexico the other. You could lie down right here and take a nice long, peaceful nap. But she knows the place and loves it, maybe even more because of the way it is. She sees Chuck's cruiser parked out front so she knows she's in luck.

Gladys sashays into Chuck's office. He looks up from whatever he was pretending to be working on and leans back in his chair. "Mornin, Gladys. Have a seat."

"I got somethin for you."

"Whats that?"

She hands the new shiny hasp to Chuck and says, "No hard feelins, I hope."

"Thank you, Gladys, course not." Chuck takes the hasp and admires it. He rummages through his desk drawer and pulls out a pad of Spriggs County official carbonless triplicate receipt tickets. Gladys is watching him, wondering what's next. "This is official business," says Chuck. "I got to write you a receipt. Just soz theres no question whats what." He scribbles a description, received on this day et cetera, tears off the original, and hands it to Gladys. "Keep this for your records. Statute of limitations on these matters is seven years."

"You mean I got to remember where this is for seven years?"

Chuck laughs. "Never know. You wouldnt want any one a these bureaucrats comin after you."

"I guess youre right." Gladys stuffs the receipt in her purse. It's only cash that goes in her brassiere. "Maybe Ill frame it when I get home."

"You might also like to know," says Chuck, "the word goin round the office this mornin is the hearin got called off." He riffles the paperwork on his desk, pulls out a folder, and goes through it. "Seeins how you moved, the Mommas in question legally no longer exists. There aint nothin left to contest, unless Enid gets the environmentalists out there investigatin the ruts you left behind. Hope you didnt run over any prairie chicken nestin areas or nothin."

"To be honest," says Gladys, "I dont think we heard the last from Weaselbomb. But maybe Im just frettin. She been so long a thorn in my side. Pretty much ever since she showed up."

"I know. Believe me, I know. Im kinda hopin the phone will be quiet now, maybe for just a day or two. I gotta say, Gladys, I admire your restraint."

"Thank you, Chuck."

"Whens your grand reopenin gonna be?"

"Not sure. Hopin before Christmas."

"Well, keep me posted. Id like to come."

"You bet. Youll be gettin a in-graved invitation!"

Chuck's pleased with this. Not always easy being the law in a small town and at the same time being friends.

Gladys stands up, so Chuck does too. "I best be goin. Lots to do," she says. They shake hands and Chuck goes to tip his hat, forgetting it's not on his head.

When Gladys gets home, she adds "fill in ruts" and "check for chicken nests, pronto," to her to-do list. Her long to-do list.

.　.　.

Dick Biotte looks up from his desk and there's Lily Calloway. Her standing in the doorway takes him by surprise every time. "Morning, Mr. Biotte," she chirps. "How are you this morning?" Every morning, right about ten, either she comes over to *The Trumpet* or Clifford goes to Dr. McNulty's office so the two can have their coffee break together.

"Good morning, Lily. I'm fine, how are you?"

"Great!" She's carrying a white paper sack, which Mr. Biotte knows has two coffees and two Danishes in it from Dickies QuickGo. His stomach grumbles; it wants coffee and Danish. "What was that?" asks Lily.

"Just my tummy," says Mr. Biotte.

"You're feeling OK?"

He smiles and nods. He looks down at his stomach, yeah, it *wants* coffee and Danish but obviously it doesn't *need* coffee and Danish.

"Well, have a great day!" says Lily. "Gotta go!"

It was so long ago, he thinks. It's been, what, twenty-one years he and his wife, Thelma, have been together. He has memories of when they were young, when they were hot for each other. Of course those memories, like the heat, have faded now. "Of course?" he asks out loud with raised eyebrows, as though dullness in life is inevitable? Wait a minute. He eyes the phone sitting on his desk. Should he call her? Why is he even wondering? This is his wife after all. How pathetic to wonder if it's OK to call your wife of twenty-one years. He picks up the phone and dials the number.

Thelma answers. "Hello?"

"It's me."

"Me? Oh! Dick! Why, you took me by surprise." Her tone shifts to one of concern. "Are you OK?"

"Oh yes, everything's fine."

"Then why are you calling?"

He shakes his head, but realizes that's not an unreasonable question. When was the last time he called his wife in the middle of the morning to say hello? He can't remember. "Was just thinking of you. Wanted to say hello."

"Are you *sure* you're OK?" she asks.

Meanwhile Lily is sitting on Clifford's desk and Clifford is tipped back in his chair agog at how stunningly beautiful she is. "What?" asks Lily, grinning sheepishly.

Clifford, abashed, nonetheless says, "I, I... Even in scrubs. You. Lily, I just think you are, Lily—"

"Hmm?" she smiles broadly.

"You're beautiful."

The two of them are thinking the same thing and spontaneously turn bright red. Lily leans toward Clifford and gives him a dainty kiss. She leans further to nibble his ear. Clifford enjoys an eyeful of her modest cleavage as she whispers, "I just wish coffee break was longer so we could go to your place." And then she sits up and smirks and watches Clifford, who is now about to faint.

Clifford gulps and squeaks, "Me too."

Cathi walks by and sneers, "You two are disgusting."

Lily looks at Clifford. When Cathi is out of earshot, she asks, "What is her problem? She *is* married, after all."

"I don't know," says Clifford. "I guess there's a difference between being married and being happily married."

"I want the happily kind," says Lily.

Clifford takes a deep breath. "So do I."

"Clifford." Mr. Biotte has appeared at his desk. "Sorry to interrupt your coffee break, you two. I have some news."

"Yes, sir?"

"Your story on Momma's got picked up by the AP."

Clifford bolts from his chair aand almost knocks Lily off the corner of his desk. "*Really, sir?*"

Mr. Biotte looks pleased as a peacock. He nods his head. Lily asks him, "What's the AP?" Mr. Biotte points to Clifford.

"It's a news service," he says. "This means my story might show up in just about any newspaper in the country."

"The world," Mr. Biotte corrects him.

Lily is beside herself. She's hopping up and down. "That's so exciting!" she squeals. She throws her arms around Clifford and gives him a kiss. "I'm so excited for you!"

"You'll have your second installment for me by the end of the day?" asks Mr. Biotte.

"Yes, sir!" snaps Clifford.

"Good. Back to work then?"

Lily looks at her watch. "Holy moly, I gotta go. Wait until Dr. McNulty hears about this!" She starts to dash for the door, stops, and rushes back to Clifford. She kisses him on the ear and whispers, "We can celebrate tonight!" She pulls back and searches Clifford's face.

Clifford smiles, looks in her eyes, and nervously nods his head.

Lily runs out and Clifford sits down. He is inspired. He has a story to tell and is completely absorbed in it when Mr. Biotte is again standing by his desk. Startled, he says, "Sir?"

"I'm going home for lunch. Could be a little late getting back."

"Are you OK, Mr. Biotte?"

"Yes, Clifford, I'm OK. Actually I'm great." With everybody's asking him if he's OK, he's thinking he might have become just a little too predictable. He's looking forward to lunch and, if he gets lucky, dessert. "And by the way, I couldn't he happier about the AP's interest in your story. Keep up the good work."

"Yes, sir. Have a good lunch."

"I will, Clifford."

Clifford notices an extra little spring in Mr. Biotte's step. Cathi pokes her head out of her cubicle and watches as he skips by. Once he's out the door, she turns to Clifford.

"Clifford?"

He pokes his head into the aisle. "Yeah?"

"You think Mr. Biotte's OK?"

.   .   .

For Thanksgiving, Clifford's off to be with his folks in Colorado and Lily heads to Michigan to be with her mom. But the two of them are the saddest creatures for better than a week before their parting, moping around, snippy, and tearful when they say good-bye.

Gladys roasts a ham for Thanksgiving dinner. No more turkey for her. Cooking a bird would only fan those memories that are too close to the surface all the time anyway. She festoons the ham with rings of pineapple, maraschino cherries, and a maple syrup glaze. Well, she uses pancake syrup, pretty much the same thing. She makes her secret green bean casserole recipe, candied yams, and a double batch of mashed potatoes. Then there's the lime jello with niblet corn and canned shrimp salad, special for Big Daddy. Nobody else will eat it. Big Daddy's in charge of pies, along with the Cool Whip, and they have Old Brucey over, who doesn't have any family left. He brings cranberry jelly, which he likes on his mashed potatoes, and the bottlebrush. Sitting at the dinner table, Old Brucey sneaks tidbits of ham to the dog, who is sitting there patiently, drooling. Gladys and Big Daddy can hear the *snap!* as it latches on to the pieces mid-air. Old Brucey sits stone faced, pretending nothing is going on.

.   .   .

Christmas and the grand reopening loom on the horizon. Step by step Big Daddy, Sam and Bill, and Clifford—when he can get away from work—put Momma's back together. They also tidy up the old lot and, as Gladys asked, make sure there are no prairie chicken nests. "Dont know why that womans so concerned about chickens all of a sudden," grumbles Big Daddy to Sam one particularly cold morning. Nor do any of them know what they'd do if they found a nest. "Cept she says Weaselbombs gonna sic the EPA on her."

"Wouldnt be a bit surprised if she did," says Sam.

Getting the two halves of the doublewide to line up and come together is more of a chore than they figured on. It takes days of tweaking and monkey business to get it together, and there's the leveling too. Get one thing set, adjust another, and the first would be out again. Finally they have the old girl snugged up and set right. The rest—setting the front steps and ramp, and hooking up the utilities—is pretty straightforward.

Gladys takes the opportunity to make a few improvements. For all the years she's been in business, she vowed to never have a TV in the place. "Destroys conversation," she says. But many of her customers have pleaded with her, whined like children even, for a TV so they can watch important events like the Superbowl or NASCAR races.

Bill in particular. "It was the Indy 500," he tells his story. "That morning my Mrs. was in town and I had chores to do around the place. We have four TVs in our trailer, so I turned em all on to the race. This way I could watch it and get my chores done at the same time. Well, my Mrs. came home and found

Indy cars screamin around ever corner of the place. She werent too pleased and didnt understand. Turned em all off and kicked me outta the house. Course that was the end of my chores, but they was only gonna wait for the next day. This is why I hope Gladysll put in a TV."

Well, Gladys decides to ease up on her policy. She gets a big screen, which Big Daddy hangs on the wall, and has the fellow come out and hook up a satellite dish. Gladys promptly tapes a sign to the screen, "For Special Events Only. For Pay (cash before the show)." She figures if customers have to pay, they'll be selective. Going home that afternoon, she notices the big dish on the roof and likes it. Makes the place look more modern, she thinks.

As a concession to the TV, she has the jukebox reprogrammed. Update it a bit, so she and the girls won't be listening to the same old songs over and over, like they have been for how many years Gladys can't remember.

Seeing how the linoleum flooring is looking pretty scruffy and then got torn up in the move, Gladys has the men pull it up and put down indoor outdoor carpet. She wanted the green color that looks like AstroTurf, but the multi-green wavy stripe motif was on sale so she went for it. "Looks good, more like the prairie in spring," she says. Big Daddy stands back and looks at the finished product and feels seasick. He refrains from comment and figures it's best just to not look at it. There's also the Put-Put Mini Golf game Grandma Bugbee picked up at a yard sale in Tulsa more than a year ago, which Gladys sets up. Something different. And the bulb in the Love Light got busted in the move, so she orders a new one out of St. Louis. "Betterin fifty dollars for that dang bulb, but we gotta have it. Special frequencies, you know," she says. "No sales tax, an shippin was free." And she puts fresh fat in the Fryolator.

The place is looking pretty good all primped up. Sam put a fresh coat of Rustoleum on the front stairs, and a little touch-up here and there on the bouncing ninnies sign. Just restock the freezer, clean the taps, and get in fresh kegs of beer and they're ready for business. And the Love Light. The free shipping might take a while.

.   .   .

Since the story got picked up, Gladys' phone is ringing off the hook. "Why I never heard of such a thing, a geriatric topless joint!" people would say. "Is it the customers or the performers thats geriatric? Whener you gonna open?" One fellow from a publishing company all the way in Vermont calls. He talks funny. "Have you thought of publishing a calendar?"

"Calendar of what?" asks Gladys.

"A pinup… pictures of your performers."

"My girls aint performers. They just tend bar an wait tables."

"I see. Even so. I think it could be a big hit."

"Mister. Do you understand my girls is all sixty-five an over? Not so pert as you might be thinkin."

"I see. Nevertheless—"

"Look, mister, I'll think about it," says Gladys. She wants to get this guy off the phone. "Right now, I got lots on my plate."

With all the purchases she's been making, Gladys maxes out her credit card. So she opens a new one that earns her frequent flier miles. Even though she isn't a frequent flier—heck, last time she got on an airplane, they all had propellers—winter is coming on fast and she figures with all the money she's spending maybe she can get her and Big Daddy a free trip. Anywhere would be fine, long as its a *warm* anywhere, thinks Gladys. Thatd be fun. Get a hotel room near the beach, with palm trees an a swimmin pool where you can wade up to a bar an have as many piña coladas as you want. All inclusive. Or maybe our own little bungalow with a thatched roof. Listen to the waves comin in, make a little love.

Gladys snaps out of her daydream. She calls Dick Biotte and puts a big ad in *The Trumpet*.

Momma's Little Harry
THE GRAND REOPENING!
(You can't keep good women down!)
Saturday Night, December 20th
All-night Drink
and Appetizer Specials
DON'T MISS IT!
(Over 21 only. We card.)

Dick says he'll fill in the corners of the ad with party balloons and trumpets and things to make it festive. Gladys knows he'll make it nice.

The weekend before the big night, Gladys, the girls, and Lily and Clifford all pitch in and give the place a much-needed scrubbing. Big Daddy and his crew make sure the freezer is stocked, and they have sufficient chips and peanuts, napkins and paper plates, and cups. They also make sure the new TV and sound system work. They have it tuned to NASCAR, and like moths to a flame the men are all drawn to it, standing there, gawking like children. Gladys walks over to Big Daddy, puts her arm around him and gives him a little peck on the cheek. He smiles, but he doesn't take his eyes off the screen.

"It all workin OK?" asks Gladys.

"Yep."

Gladys slyly slips the remote out of Big Daddy's hand. "You fellers got any more chores to tend to?"

Big Daddy, transfixed by the cars going round and round, silently nods his head yes.

Gladys hits the power button and the screen instantly goes black.

"Hey! What all?" pleads Big Daddy. Bill and Sam are equally befuddled. "What happened?"

"You fellers can read the sign, cant you?"

"But, but—"

"No buts. You all an we all still got work to do." Gladys stuffs the remote down into her cleavage with a perfunctory push. The men skulk away in different directions, grumbling, muttering "but that was *NASCAR.*" Gladys thinks the TV might not have been such a good idea.

Big Daddy gets the stepladder, fixing to put the new bulb in the Love Light.

"Honeybunch?" he asks Gladys, "Where's that new high frequency pink bulb you got?"

"On the shelf with the pool balls," she hollers from behind the bar. Gladys is in the middle of removing a well mummified mouse carcass from under the prep sink. "Disgusting!" she hisses.

"What?" asks Big Daddy.

"Not you. Its a damn dead mouse Im dealin with."

Big Daddy plucks the bulb from the shelf. It's in a special high tech package. One of those it takes two men and a boy with sharp power tools to get into. He notices the price sticker ($52.95), raises his eyebrows, and shakes his head. He suddenly realizes he got into the wrong line of work. He studies the package, turning it around and around, trying to figure out how to open it. He can see the glittering pink bulb in there. He just can't get to it. So he takes out his multi-tool and starts prying at one edge. He pries, then he opens a blade and he cuts, taking care not to stab himself. Then he pries some more, but he's getting close to nowhere. He's got a little edge torn up is all he's got. Again he opens the pliers and starts yanking on it. He's getting frustrated. This aint a goddamned nuclear weapon, its just a friggin light bulb, he thinks. And he yanks on it and twists and finally... POP! The bulb goes flying. Big Daddy is gripped by fear. No! He can't let anything happen to that bulb. $52.95, shipped in special from St. Louis. Gladys'd skin him! He keeps his eye on the bulb and makes a lunge. He crashes onto the new wavy green carpeting, and the doublewide shakes. Big Daddy flashes back to his days in high school football. His hand is extended. He slides. He keeps his eye on the bulb, and *plink!* It lands ever so softly into the cup of his palm.

"Everthin OK?" hollers Gladys. She pops up from behind the bar and glares at him. "What all is goin on?"

Big Daddy lays there and breathes. "Ever... thins... OK. Honeybunch."

"What all er you doin layin there?"

"Just thinkin." What he's thinking about is the damn bulb better work.

"Some days," says Gladys, "I just cant figger men out."

Big Daddy thinks to himself, good, hope we can keep it that way. The day she can figger me out, the day its gonna be trouble. He slowly labors back up to his feet. He can feel it in his shoulder. Not as young as he used to be. He climbs the ladder and with his big burly stubs of fingers plugs in the new bulb. He turns and there's Puss N. Boots standing watching him.

"Puss, would you all do me a favor an switch on the Love Light?"

"My pleasure," she purrs. Puss throws the switch and instantly the room is bathed in beautiful, loving, special from St. Louis, pink wavelengths of light.

"Well looky there," says Big Daddy. "By golly, I can feel the Love!"

Gladys steps around the bar wiping her hands on a towel. "Mm... my man. We all can feel the Love." She gives Big Daddy a wet smack on the cheek, and his face lights up. "Mm... therell be somethin special for you tonight."

"Mee-ow!" says Puss as she claws the air.

Lily steps out from cleaning the ladies room. "Clifford?" she calls.

"Hello?" Clifford calls back. He puts the last keg of beer in the fridge, turns, and there's Lily. She presses her lips to his and gives him a long, passionate kiss.

"I can feel it!" she croons. "Feel the Love, Clifford?"

After a kiss like that, so unexpected, so full of promise, "Uh-huh" is the best he can manage. They all bask in the pink glow. It does seem to have an effect.

Gladys looks at her watch. "I say its time to blow the quittin whistle. Lets have us a beer an celebrate a little before the hordes descend upon us." She turns to Clifford. "Any one a those kegs tapped yet?"

"No, ma'am."

"Well why dont you take your pick and hook er up. I got a little surprise, a new item, on the appetizer menu. Time to try it out." Clifford goes back to the refrigerator to hook up a keg, Gladys heads for the kitchen, and Puss starts pulling out glasses. She looks around for a bar towel, and not finding one untucks her T-shirt to give each glass a polish. Lily is watching Big Daddy and trying her best not to laugh out loud as he occupies himself with the mini put-put golf game. His great lumbering hulk tippy-toeing around in the miniature dreamland golf course.

"Should be ready to draw a glass," calls Clifford from the refrigerator. "The amber ale."

"Got it," calls Puss. She tips a glass up to the tap, but most of what comes out is foam. She sets the glass aside and pours another. The aroma of hot fat, smooth and rich, wafts from the kitchen. For a moment, sounds of mad bubbling as frozen food hits hot fat fills the room. Gladys is cooking up her surprise.

Puss pours the beers and lines them up on the bar, each glistening glass with a perfect foamy head. Gladys comes out of the kitchen with four red plastic baskets stacked up her left arm, each lined with white parchment paper that's already grease soaked, each basket is filled with, well, it's hard to say what they are filled with. Everyone gathers around, eyeing the crispy contents. They look like giant French fries, but then again, they don't. Big Daddy's about to grab one.

"Hold it," says Gladys. "First a toast." She and Puss hand the glasses of beer around, then Gladys clears her throat. "I couldnt a done it without you. Each and ever one of you." She looks around at the smiling faces, Big Daddy, Puss, Bill, Sam, Grandma Bugbee, Lily, and Clifford. She raises her glass. "Heres to you and my little Harry." Solemnly they raise their glasses and everyone takes a sip.

"Heres to Mommas Little Harry!" caws Big Daddy. They all join in and take long draws on their beers.

"Now, everbody," says Gladys as she pulls a tissue out from her sleeve and blows her nose. "Try my little surprise. Tell me what you all think. An be honest."

Big Daddy doesn't hesitate. He grabs a spear and crunches into it. A look of complete bewilderment comes over his face. He studies the bitten-off end of what he's left holding. It's vaguely green. Like a flock of hawks, everyone's watching him. "Well, I... I never had anythin like it."

"What are they?" asks Lily.

Bill and Sam and everybody else looks at Gladys. "Theys the latest thing. Deep-fried dill pickles! Makin waves all cross the Midwest!" She gazes lovingly at Big Daddy. "What all do you think?"

He's munching on the second half. "Theys good. Different, but good." He takes a gulp from his beer. "Id take a nuther one." Then Bill takes one, then Lily, and then they're all munching on deep-fried dill pickles.

Gladys watches approvingly. "Well, it just got awful quiet. I guess thats a good sign." She reaches for a spear. "Spect Ill try one now."

"You made us try them first?" asks Clifford.

"Well, yeah. You didnt think I was gonna eat one without makin sure they was OK!" cackles Gladys, her eyes twinkling. "How bout now I make us some buffalo wings?" Without waiting for an answer, she's off to the kitchen.

"Always wondered what part a the buffalo they made those things from, " says Sam. "I mean, they sure as heck look like chicken wings to me. Taste like em too."

Grandma Bugbee stares at him in disbelief. "You old fool, they is chicken wings!"

"Well, whynt they call em that then, if youre so smartypants!" demands Sam, doing his best to look dignified.

"Now you two, don get started," growls Puss. "Sam, its what they call *marketing*."

"Well, I never heard a such a thing," says Sam, pouting. "Makin part of a chicken out to be part of a dang buffalo." He

144

sips his beer. "You never heard em call a pork chop a *chicken chop* now did you?"

"Sam!" Puss puts her fists on her hips. "Just dont worry your poor little head over it." She looks around and meows, "Anybody for a little game a pool?"

"Youre on," says Big Daddy.

"Oh, this otta be good," Grandma hisses to Clifford. "Ol Puss knows her way around the table."

"Eightball, Big Daddy?" purrs Puss. "Dollar a ball?"

"Thems high stakes," whispers Grandma. "Big Daddys gonna take a hosin."

"Sure, Puss," says Big Daddy as he struts over to the table. They flip a coin for break, and it goes to Big Daddy. "Chivalry is not dead," he says. "Puss, you break." By now, Big Daddy should know better. He's taken a whipping from Puss before, but he can't help it.

"Why thank you Big Daddy. I jus *love*," meows Puss, "playin with a *gentleman*." Big Daddy is a complete sucker for a little tease and Puss knows it. Puss breaks and purposely flubs it up.

Big Daddy, now a picture of concentration, takes his shot and pockets the solid three ball. He looks up from the table, pleased as a peacock. "Two dollars if you call the shot?" he asks.

Puss simply nods her head.

Big Daddy eyes the table. "Two ball side pocket." He takes his shot and misses. He examines his cue stick like there's something wrong with it, then chalks the tip and has a seat. Puss studies the table. She has stripes.

"Buffalo wings, everbody!" announces Gladys as she lays four baskets of hot sizzling wings on the bar. Big Daddy gets up and puts three on a plate, then helps himself to some ranch dressing.

Puss points to the far corner pocket with her cue stick and says, "Four ball." She puts a little reverse English on the cue ball, and sinks the four. She calls her next shot and makes it. Big Daddy sits down dejectedly, while Puss, just because she can, calls her shots and one by one clears the table. All except the eight ball. It's her last shot and it's going to be a tough one, a bank shot to the side, and on top of it, the eight sits right next to the pocket.

"Miss this one, Puss," says Big Daddy, looking smug. He devours a wing.

"I know," says Puss. "Or sink the cue ball." Puss doesn't like this at all. In her catly way, she circles the table. She comes around and points to the side pocket next to her. She has to bounce the cue ball off the opposing bank and sink the eight ball without having the cue ball follow it into the pocket.

Big Daddy nonchalantly continues munching. He purposely smacks his lips; otherwise you could hear a pin drop. Puss waits. Big Daddy stops smacking. Puss takes her shot. Everyone holds their breath. The cue ball rolls across the table, hits the bank, rolls back across the table, and hits the eight ball, which drops into the side pocket. The cue ball keeps rolling, heading for the same pocket. Slowly, slowly, it approaches the edge of the pocket. Big Daddy is hoping for a favorable tailwind. All eyes are on the white ball. It slows and finally, right on the edge, with only a hair to go, it stops.

The crowd erupts into hoots and cheers. Puss stands there, smiles demurely, and looks around. The cue ball sits there. "Next?" is all she says.

Oddly enough, she has no takers.

.   .   .

Everything is set for the grand reopening. Nonetheless, Gladys fidgets. She paces, she doesn't sleep well, and she drives Big Daddy nuts. What if it snows? Maybe she should have ordered an extra bulb for the Love Light. And it's been just too quiet with Weaselbomb. Old Brucey saw her when he and the bottlebrush were out for a walk, but she scurried by, didn't even say hello. No one's heard a peep from her, and this more than anything gives Gladys cause for concern.

One evening Big Daddy is at Gladys' to watch a movie. He's been thinking he wants to do something special for her, given all she's been through with moving Momma's. Seeing that Christmas is right around the corner, he says, "Honeybunch, Id like to get a string a Christmas lights for the front a Mommas, just make it that much more festive for her grand reopenin."

Gladys, ensconced in the La-Z-Boy, isn't looking too good. Kind of pale and worn out. She smiles and says, "Why Big Daddy, thats sweet a you to offer. Thatd be mighty nice, but frankly I dont got it in me to do any more."

"Dont you worry none. Thisll be my treat. What color you want?"

"Oh, Honeybuns, whatever all you decide on will be fine." Big Daddy smiles, and Gladys thinks soon as she said this it might have been a mistake. Big Daddy isn't known for having the most refined taste in the world. But he looks so pleased sittin there, Gladys is happy to just let him be.

"Well, Ill take good care of it. Everbodyll know Santas comin to town!" Big Daddy pats the sofa next to where hes sitting. "Cmon. Why dont you come over here an well snuggle under the comforter while we watch the movie."

"That means I have to get up."

"Cmon, you old woman." Big Daddy knows this will get to her. He can see the flash of fire in her eyes and he can't help but start giggling.

"What er you laughin at?" Gladys asks as she cranks herself out of the recliner.

"Nuthin." Big Daddy reaches over and grabs the comforter. Gladys plops herself down close beside him with a grunt and a sigh and Big Daddy spreads the comforter over them.

Gladys leans in against him. "I love you with all my ol heart," she says, smiling.

"An I love you too," replies Big Daddy as he wraps his arm around her and she snuggles in even closer. He turns on the TV and starts the movie. Not ten minutes into it, Gladys is sound asleep, breathing steadily. And not ten minutes later, Big Daddy is asleep too.

Next morning, Big Daddy goes to the feed store. Clyde's there, curious and nosey as ever. He's wearing a sweater with a Santa Claus knitted into the front. Big Daddy looks at it. He wouldn't wear a sweater like that to a dog fight. "Well good morning, Ru— I mean Big Daddy," says Clyde. He's known Big Daddy most all his life as Rupert Twitchit, and he still has the hardest time not calling him that. "Havent seen you in here quite a while. What all you been doin with yourself? I heard about the big move. Pretty clever if I do say so."

"Oh Im sure you have said so." Big Daddy knows Clyde doesn't mean any harm, but still the little busybody just bugs him. "Clyde, wheres your Christmas lights?"

"Decided not to carry em this year."

"What?" Big Daddy is incredulous. "No Christmas lights?"

"Nope. Cant compete with the big stores in Boise City."

"You mean to tell me people will drive sixty miles to save what, two dollars on a string a Christmas lights?"

"Yep. Happens ever day."

There are times, and this is one of them, when Big Daddy fails to understand the human race. "So no Christmas lights. None."

"Ye—wait a minute. Hold yer horses, lemme check out back. We might just have a string left over from last year. Ill be right back."

Big Daddy loiters around the counter. He studies the transistor radio hanging from the window crank; it has a bent coat hanger stuck in it for an antenna. It crackles and hums and the local AM station is playing a sad country song of lost love. He looks over the displays. Elkskin ropers, alfalfa cubes, tins of Bag Balm, Reese's Cups, bottles of saddle soap. This place has always done a good business. You think the least they could do is carry some Christmas lights. Clyde comes skipping back carrying a dusty box.

"Its your lucky day!" he cries.

Big Daddy thinks to himself oh yeah it sure as hell is. "What color is the lights?" he asks.

Clyde takes a deep breath and blows the dust and bits of hay off the box, right into Big Daddy's face. Big Daddy starts sneezing, thinking Clyde has all the sense of a tree stump. Clyde looks up. "Oh, sorry bout that." He examines the box, turns it over and around. "Ah, here it is! Theys purple." Clyde spits on the end of the box. "Nothin like a little spit!" he says and wipes it with his sleeve. "See? Says right here. 'Purple.' An this one got the 'Optional Cascading Strobe Feature.' Look, it says, 'Spice Up Your Christmas!' See, says right here." Clyde points excitedly at the description on the box.

Big Daddy figures purple might not be too Christmassy, but it sure beats a trip to Boise City. And with the trailer's painted trim, it could just end up working out real nice. "How much?" he asks.

"Regular price is $24.99. Well let you have em half price. Hows that?"

"Ill take em." Big Daddy grabs a two-pack of King Size Reese's Cups. "Ill take these too."

As Big Daddy's driving back through town, he notices Lily carrying a white paper sack into *The Trumpet*. Must be bringing Clifford a morning coffee. That boy Clifford is one good kid and a lucky son of a gun, thinks Big Daddy. He stops at Dickies for a few items and then heads home. Driving along, munching on his Reese's Cups, he's thinking Gladys is gonna be some kind a pleased with the lights, an the strobe feature really otta liven things up, specially with the neon ninnies.

After putting away his groceries, he gets his staple gun and an extension cord out of the work shed and walks over to Momma's with the lights. Who should he bump into but Weaselbomb. Even though it's cold and looking like snow, Big Daddy starts to sweat. He just doesn't like this woman. Nonetheless he's polite, which if nothing else is good Karma. "Good morning, Enid," he says. "How are you doin?"

"Dont try to sweet-talk me Rupert!" squawks Weaselbomb.

"Just tryin to be neighborly," says Big Daddy. He can't help but grind his teeth. "Nothin more."

Weaselbomb eyes him suspiciously. "Im well, Rupert. Does that answer your question?"

"Yes it does. I spect Ill be on my way." Big Daddy starts walking.

"Not so quick!"

150

Big Daddy cringes and pauses for a moment. He wonders if there's anything in this universe that'd please this woman. He shudders at the thought, and turns to face the little pain in the— no, no, he thinks, remain civil. "Yes, Enid, what is it?"

"What you got in the box?"

"Christmas lights. Shouldnt be a bother to you. Not now."

"You dont need to get snide," hisses Weaselbomb. "You know Im, oh, never mind. What I care bout never has been or ever will be of importance to you and your kind. I spect youre going to further decorate that, that den of iniquity. You go right ahead."

"Enid, I hope you have a nice day." Big Daddy turns to take his leave. He feels like he's turning his back on a snapping dog, wondering what part of him is likely to get bit.

"Nice day? Ha!" says Enid as she turns abruptly and goes on her way.

Big Daddy is still rattled by the time he gets to Momma's. He takes three deep breaths and sets down to figuring out what he's going to do with the lights. He lays them out on the front walkway and plugs them in. Oh yeah, they're purple all right, and they're bright and they're strobing to beat the band. He's getting dizzy looking at them, so he pulls the plug. No wonder they were left over from last year. What the heck, he thinks as he staples the lights so they follow the curvy purple stripe, and when they're strobing, they'll point customers to the door. He's just about to plug them in when Gladys walks up the steps.

"I just love a man whos good with his hands." She's dressed in her winter jacket with artificial fur lined collar, and tights and high boots. "My *handy* man."

Big Daddy looks up and grins, "I just love it when you dress up," he says. She gives him a lascivious look. Big Daddy feels his knees weaken, feels a certain tightening. He thinks, dang its hard to get anythin done with this woman around. But he's enjoying every moment of having those strong womanly gams planted in front of him.

.   .   .

In the early murk of Saturday morning, Gladys and Big Daddy, bleary eyed, are drinking coffee at the table in the breakfast nook. This is the big day, the day Momma's Little Harry will reopen in all her glory. Neither of them has slept well, Gladys hasn't slept well all week. A few flakes of snow spit from the sky and streak sideways in a bitter north wind. Gladys looks out the window.

"I dont like the looks a this," she says. "Forecast is for three to five inches. Could ruin everthin."

Big Daddy reaches over and rubs Gladys' shoulder. He searches her tired face. "Honeybunch, we take what comes. Dont make no difference how many shows up. Its gonna be a fine time. Dont worry."

Gladys turns and seeing Big Daddy's big old mug, a face with kindness written all over it, says, "Oh Sweetums, Im just the luckiest girl I know." Big Daddy grabs tissues from the box and hands them to her. He knows what's coming. Gladys honks her nose and blubbers on. "You been so good to me. None a us, we couldnt a done this without you."

Using his big old thumbs, Big Daddy gently wipes the tears off Gladys' cheeks. He runs his hands over her shoulders and leans in and gives her a kiss on the forehead. "My old woman, thats what were all here for. Aint one of us alone has to carry the whole world on our shoulders. Everthin will be fine. Youll see."

"Im just so tired. Guess I aint so young as I used to be. Aint thinkin straight no more."

Big Daddy smiles. "We all in the same boat." He sips his coffee. "How bout I make us some breakfast, an then we get on with the day?"

Meanwhile at Clifford's place, Clifford and Lily are beginning to stir. Lily rolls over, snuggles into Clifford's side, and presses her breasts against him. Clifford slowly opens his eyes and seeing Lily he smiles. "Good morning, Sweetheart," she says.

"Hmm, makes me so happy to wake up and see you," says Clifford. He tucks his arm under Lily's neck and draws her even closer. She wraps herself around him, and their warmth radiates under the covers. The bed is filled with the earthy scents of their loving.

"Today's the big day," says Lily. "You ready for it?"

"I don't know. Never been in a topless bar before."

"Just don't get any ideas, Clifford Bagsley."

Clifford guffaws. "Sweetheart, there's nothing to worry about." He rubs Lily's back. He thinks about Gladys and her girls. Any one of them is old enough to be his mother, grandmother even." He furrows his brow. "Going to be kind of strange, actually."

Lily giggles. "Yeah. All those old titties. Gravity, you know."

"Got to hand it to them. In a manner of speaking," says Clifford and the two of them fall into hoots of laughter.

"What time are we heading over?"

"I told Gladys we'd show up around five. Help with whatever last minute-things come up."

"Good." says Lily. "So there's no rush." She presses into Clifford, who can feel a wave of heat flowing from her body. He can feel his own heat too. He rolls onto his side, faces Lily, runs his hand down her side to her hips, and draws her to him.

. . .

The waffles pop out of the toaster. Big Daddy makes a sport out of catching them mid-air. He sets the two on a plate beside the heap of crispy bacon slices, and rushes it to the table for Gladys. "Get em while theys hot! You got yer oleo an syrup right here."

Gladys looks up at him, still a little teary. "Thank you, Honeybuns." She slathers the oleo onto the waffles, each little square hole is filled and turning to liquid. She then pours on the syrup, thinking to herself about the day ahead. Big Daddy places a fresh pot of coffee on the table. He returns with his plate and sits down, goes for the oleo and syrup and gets down to business.

"Funny how it is," says Gladys, "Im more worked up about this reopenin than I was seven years ago with the openin-openin. Guess its this whole mess with Weaselbomb."

Big Daddy finishes chewing his mouthful of waffles. "Only thing we have to fear, Honeybunch, is fear itself." He cuts off another chunk of waffle and picks up a strip of bacon. Waving it like a pointer, he says, "Somebody more famous an smart than me said that, so it must be true." He stuffs the whole strip of bacon in his mouth.

Gladys looks at him, smiles, and shakes her head. "You are somethin. Got more horse sense than any one a them famous people. *Smart* people. Smart *and* famous people." She sighs in satisfaction and eats her breakfast. Running her finger around the plate to get the last bit of oleo and syrup, she says, "That were good, Honeybuns." She licks her finger, and then stands up. "Ill do the dishes," she says as she starts clearing the table. Big Daddy drains the last of the coffee into his mug, grounds and all, and sips the cup.

When he brings his plate into the kitchen, Gladys is at the sink with her arms up to her elbows in hot sudsy water. Big Daddy presses himself up behind her, slips his plate into the hot water, and draws his hands up Gladys' arms. "Mm... you Big Devil, you," she murmurs. Big Daddy kisses her neck, Gladys coos. "Im... this is... we otta have us a little mornin delight. Maybe youd like to warm up the covers while I finish these dishes?"

Big Daddy growls into her ear like an old Tom and runs his soapy hands up under her breasts. He gives her a little love bite. "That sounds like the best ideer yet."

"Lord knows, there aint gonna be nothin left tonight!" says Gladys.

Big Daddy's under the covers when Gladys comes in. She slips out of her fuzzy robe and in between the sheets by her man. He's ready for her. "Mm, thats fine," she whispers as she wriggles close to him, feels him. "Mighty fine."

They make slow and tender love, and then snooze for a while. The first sound sleep either of them have had in days. Gladys wakes with a start, she sits up and looks at the clock. It's eleven. She leans over and kisses Big Daddy on the cheek. "Honeybuns, we got to git on with it."

Big Daddy slowly comes to life. "I spose," he mutters. He rolls over and looks at Gladys. "That was nice. Nice start to a big day."

Gladys hauls her old body out of the bed and showers. Big Daddy gets up and puts on his T-shirt and drawers. He sticks his head in the shower. "Honeybunch, Im headed over to my place to get cleaned up."

"Ill be headed over to Mommas," says Gladys. "Turn the heat up, an make sure everthins OK. Whynt you come over when you can."

.   .   .

Gladys dresses in her coveralls and heads over to Momma's. There's a dusting of snow on the ground, but the clouds are thinning. "Prayers answered," she calls to the sky. "Thank you, Lord."

Here and there, dots of sunshine race across the prairie. Might just clear up to be a nice day. She sees Old Brucey walking the bottlebrush. Gladys thinks to herself these two make quite the pair—the old Hungarian all bundled up, and his scraggly little dog. In spite of its little tartan plaid sweater, the dog stands there and shakes.

"Good morning, Gladys," calls Old Brucey. "Mother Nature it seems, she is doing us a favor!"

"Yes, good morning, Brucey." The fresh air, the breaking weather, thoughts of her loving man. Gladys is feeling much better. "How are you?" she asks.

"Not bad for an old Hunky."

The bottlebrush sniffs intently at Gladys' pant leg. "Hes not gonna piss on me, is he?"

"I hope not," says Old Brucey. He gives the bottlebrush's lead a little tug, but the dog stands firm and continues to sniff. Gladys moves away, and the dog follows. "Are you ready for the big day?" Brucey asks as he raises his collar against the wind.

"Ready as Ill ever be." says Gladys.

"From what I hear, the grand reopening is the big event of the year. I cannot wait!"

"Me neither. Part of me cant wait for it just to be over."

"Ahh, Gladys. All will go well," Old Brucey reassures her. "You will see." He gives the bottlebrush a little tug. "Come on, old friend. Too cold to sniff forever!"

"See you tonight," says Gladys.

"Indeed." Old Brucey tips his hat, bows to Gladys, and is on his way. Slowly though, as the bottlebrush loiters here and there.

Gladys is relieved to see no sign of foul play at Momma's. She unlocks the door, steps in, and locks the door behind her. It's dim inside, and other than the wind rattling the kitchen vent, it's quiet. She turns on the Love Light and turns the heat up to eighty. Heat is one thing you got to have if you're walking around all night without a shirt on. The furnace clicks and ticks and finally begins to blow, cold air at first, then warm. Shafts of sunlight flash in the windows and race across the floor, then disappear. Gladys' hope of hopes is for the snow to hold off. She walks around, absorbed in her thoughts and memories. There's really little to do except wait and fuss. She checks the restrooms, they're clean as whistles. Gladys then putters into the kitchen and sets the Fryolator on low. It takes a while to heat up all that cold fat. She eyes the fire extinguisher—the little pointer in the gauge is in the green zone.

Gladys hopes Chuck will show up, just in case there's any trouble. She thinks about calling him but decides not to interrupt his day off. A rattle at the door startles her, she practically jumps. To her relief, it's Big Daddy. He ambles in.

As he's taking off his jacket, he asks, "Hows my woman?"

"Tired, scared, excited," says Gladys.

Big Daddy gives her a bear hug. "Everthins gonna be all right."

Gladys hears commotion out front, and then a knock at the door. "Would you get it?" she asks Big Daddy.

"Sure." He goes to the door and peers out. It's the girls. He opens the door and swings it wide. "Cmon in!"

Grandma Bugbee, Puss N. Boots, and Miss Bunny clamber in. They're all bubbly and excited. Miss Bunny flew in special, into Amarillo from North Dak for the weekend. The girls kept her coming as a surprise for Gladys.

"Well I declare!" hoots Gladys. "Miss Bunny!"

The floor of the doublewide shakes under Bunny's footfalls as she runs to Gladys and throws her arms around her. Bunny picks her right up off the floor and swings her around like a rag doll. And Gladys is not a particularly small woman.

"Whoo-EE!" squeals Gladys, "But be careful. Im gittin to be a old lady, kinda rickety you know."

Miss Bunny gently sets her down and gives her a big kiss on the cheek. "Im some kinda pleased to see you! How all you been? Your healths good?" Bunny stands back and in her cross-eyed way, appraises Gladys up and down. "Girl, youre sure lookin good!"

Having Miss Bunny show up brightens Gladys' day considerably, the others chime in and they get to chattering and catching up, girlfriends that they all are. "Wait til you see my new costume," says Miss Bunny. "No, I aint gonna even give a hint. Its gonna be a surprise."

"You, girl, are just full a surprises." says Gladys.

Big Daddy stands back, smiles, and soaks in all the chatter. He's happy to see Gladys so excited, just like the ol Gladys before all the trouble. It warms his heart.

158

The commotion dies down and Gladys announces, "Girls, I best be goin home an maybe take a little nap. Its gonna be a big night. A *big* night! An you all rest up too. We gonna have some fun, Mommas style. Just like ol times. Im so glad were all together!"

.   .   .

Feeling refreshed after her snooze, Gladys gets herself ready to go. She'll be wearing a Mrs. Claus outfit, with a red sequined bodice that makes her ninnies stand up like they were younger, a green mini-skirt, and bright red spike heel boots. She'll also wear her red velvet gloves and a Santa Claus hat. Getting dressed and looking at herself in the mirror, she's feeling better and better. Admiring herself this way and that, she says, "After all these years, girl, you still got the goods."

Big Daddy comes by dressed as Mr. Claus. He takes a good look at Gladys, his jaw drops. "Dang, woman. Whatever presents you be handin out, save one for me!"

Gladys looks at him and flutters her eyelashes. "Theres always presents for you. Long as you been good."

"I been good, I promise," says Big Daddy.

Gladys puts on her overcoat and Mr. and Mrs. Claus get into the Toronado and make for Momma's. What's already parked out front when they get there but a van with fancy lettering all over it and a big satellite dish on top pointed to the heavens. "Lord sakes!" exclaims Gladys. "Its KOK TV outta Oklahoma City!" With authority, Big Daddy wheels the Toronado up next to it. Immediately, a reporter and film crew descend upon them. Gladys looks at Big Daddy and says, "This is how it is on TV with movie stars." Her eyes are twinkling. "But this time its us. We must be famous!" The horde sweeps over to Gladys' side of the car. Big Daddy gets out, adjusts his costume, and swaggers around to open the door for her. If ever there was a time to be a gentleman, this is it.

"Stand back, please," Big Daddy says with authority as he opens the car door.

"Gladys Calloway?" asks the reporter, a trim young man in a charcoal tweed wool overcoat. His hair is perfect.

Gladys looks up. She squints in the bright camera lights. "What all is that?"

The reporter glances up. "Oh, that's the microphone on a boom. You don't have to pay any attention to it. Mrs. Calloway, we'd like to get—"

"Make that Gladys. Everbody calls me Gladys. An Im one busy woman right now." Big Daddy helps her out of the car and swings the door hard to close it. The hinges creak and gronk. He has to slam it twice to get it to catch. Gladys' spikes sink into the prairie, making things a bit wobbly and awkward.

The reporter waves the crew in closer. "Mrs. Gladys, rather, Gladys, I'm John Masterson with KOK TV. We're *live*, on the scene at, er," he looks at his note cards, "Momma's Little Harry. Harry. Harry? Yes, folks, that's it."

The boom operator hovers the mic just above Gladys' head. She looks up at it. "Could you all git that danglin... *member* outta my face? Id preciate it."

John Masterson's eyes go wide. The boom operator raises the mic slightly.

Gladys warms up to the reporter. "Yep, so far you got it right. This youre seein here is the Grand Reopenin of Mommas Little Harry. Nice of you all to—"

"This must be an exciting moment for you. We're here for the inside story."

"Oh, youre not gettin inside a Mommas Little Harry with them cameras an all. Its not zactly family material." With

160

this, Gladys gives John a big wink and continues. "Its for a *mature* audience. John, you can come in when we open an Ill treat you to a beer and my special deep-fried dill pickle spears. If you like."

"Thank you, Gladys. But why a *re*opening?"

"We had a problem with a so-called neighbor. More of a pain in the ass, actually."

John glances at the cameras and smiles apologetically. "Anyway," Gladys continues, "she werent too happy, so we moved Mommas to its *new* location, an now weez gonna reopen her up. Should be quite a time."

"Gladys, what about your girls. They'll be here?"

"Oh yeah. Grandma Bugbee, Puss N. Boots, an Miss Bunny, all the way from Fargo, North Dak. They be here shortly. You be sure to say hello. Look, John, I gots to get to work. You be sure to come in later. My treat, but no cameras inside. Understand?"

"You bet." The reporter looks at the camera. "This is John Masterson, *live* at the grand reopening of Momma's Little Harry."

In the middle of what he's saying, Gladys leans over and gives him a wet smacky kiss on the cheek, leaving a big red lipstick print behind. John Masterson blushes, and cries, "Cut!" to his cameramen.

With the camera crew in tow, Gladys and Big Daddy make their way to Momma's front door. Gladys turns to the cameras—she's loving the attention—and blows them a kiss. Once they're inside she says to Big Daddy, "Be sure to lock the door. Them pappakuzzi can wait like everbody else." Gladys turns on the neon sign and plugs in the purple strobe-effect Christmas lights. "There. That otta get em excited!" She goes around and lowers all the shades, then turns on the Love Light.

She cranks up the Fryolator. Big Daddy is behind the bar, checking things. Nervously, he polishes a few glasses.

Gladys stands in the main room surveying the scene. "Guess theres not much to do. What time is it?"

Big Daddy checks his watch. "Five twenty."

"Come here for a sec, Honeybuns."

Big Daddy glances up. He walks around the end of the bar with an expectant look on his face. Slowly, teasingly, Gladys unbuttons her overcoat and pushes it off her shoulders.

"Oh my. Lordy, *Lordy*," whispers Big Daddy.

Gladys lets the coat drop to the floor.

"Honeybunch…" Big Daddy's choked up. "There was a time I feared I might never see you, this… agin."

Gladys lowers her chin, coquettishly cocks her head, and smiles. She extends a hand and curls her index finger. "Come here, Big Boy. We got a private moment."

Big Daddy approaches her, places his hands on her hips, leans down, and kisses her breasts. Gladys places her hands on Big Daddy's head, arches her back, and draws in a deep passionate breath. "Mm, my *Big* Boy." There's a knock at the door. "Damn it." she mutters.

Big Daddy straightens himself. Smiling like a cat, he asks, "Shall I get the door, Madam?"

Gladys swats at him and giggles. "I aint no Madam!"

It's the girls hamming it up with the camera crew swarming around them. Big Daddy lets the girls in. He peeks out the door, there's cars parked around and people waiting. John Masterson is busy interviewing folks. With the bright lights it looks like a carnival. Big Daddy spots Chuck Dalhart in the crowd and is glad to see him. He closes the door and makes sure to lock it. "Theres a crowd out there," he says. "I bet morin forty people." Gladys and the girls look at one another. "Gonna be a big night!"

There's another knock at the door, it's Lily and Clifford. Big Daddy lets them in, and this time the crowd is at the door. He pushes them back, shouting "Sorry, not open til six!" There's grumbles of disappointment.

Inside, Lily and Clifford collect themselves. "We got *interviewed*," says Lily, primly.

"Us too!" chime the girls.

Clifford averts his eyes. He can't quite bring himself to look at Gladys, standing there with her titties sticking out. Gladys laughs. "Cliff, you aint seen nothin yet!" She turns to the girls. "I think its showtime!" Starting with Puss, the girls disrobe. Clifford's holding his breath, and Lily, at his side, has a worried look on her face. She clutches his arm. Gladys describes the girls' outfits like they were haute couture on a runway.

"Miss Boots slinks outta her overcoat an meows like the hot pussycat she is. Her outfit, what there is of it, is black vinyl. She sportin high pirate boots with golden buckles an the cuffs turned down, a bikini bottom with a long an sultry cat tail, evenin gloves up to her elbows with claws on the fingertips. She tops it off with a tricorne hat. Her eyes flash like tiger agates, she has silky whiskers, an shes wearin a choker an low-slung belt a gold coins."

"Them coins is imitation," whispers Puss. She wraps her clawed hands under her breasts, lifts them, and meows.

Gladys continues, "Once in costume an on the floor, she dont speak a word. Its all meows an growls an purrs, an if a customer gets too frisky there could be some hissin an spittin. Not a one of em has yet failed to get the message: Hands off!"

Clifford gawks and his mouth hangs open. Speechless, he swallows hard. Lily is horrified but intrigued. She glances at

Clifford and whispers, "Would you ever want me to dress up like that?"

Clifford stammers, "Um, no! Well, um, no!"

"Next, Grandma Bugbee shows us herself," continues Gladys. Grandma carefully removes her hat, revealing her silver blonde hair combed back in a tight bun and held in place with pink barrettes. She drops her coat to the floor. "Shes wearin ruffled cuffs," says Gladys, "rings a silver an gold on her fingers, a light pink short sleeve cardigan with a very, *very* low-cut neck line, a shimmerin hot pink thong with print gingham miniskirt apron an ruffled trim, an sensible brown pumps. Her deep blue eyes twinkle, she has red rouge dots on er cheeks, complementin the bleedin blue tat by her left eye. Rockin Grandma! Customers love bein naughty, so shell threaten em with a spankin."

"An a course we have Miss Bunny. Theres been hints her costume is all new. Everones been waitin, the anticipation for what shell be wearin is red hot. Bunny is big, even she'll tell you that," says Gladys. Bunny shakes her head of blonde tangles and puts on a football helmet. Off comes her jacket. "Shes wearin a short-cut football jersey, with a peek-a-boo panel a clear vinyl sewn into the front with what looks like TV controls embroidered beneath it."

"Its my big-screen," says Bunny. "I know, big girl, small titties, but I still like em."

"Shes wearin short shorts an cleated field shoes with team color athletic socks." Big Daddy is agaw. He likes watching a game now and then. Gladys sucks her teeth. "Girl, you are hot. I like where all youre goin." She sees Clifford looking like a horse in a fire. "What do you think, Cliff?" asks Gladys. "Puss got your tongue? Or is it the Bunny?"

"Um. Er. No. Well I, I—" The girls all start giggling. Clifford turns red, "I, I, I guess I'll see what I can do to help in the kitchen!" He rushes away and the girls, except Lily, all think this is the funniest thing they've ever seen.

"Time to get down to business," announces Gladys. She looks at Big Daddy. "Maybe we otta open that door before they break it down. Girls, you all ready? Anybody got to pee?"

No one speaks up. Puss growls sweetly. "Well, then. Now everbody, remember," says Gladys, "Sam, Bill, Angel, an Old Brucey, whatever they want is on the house." She collects herself and takes a deep breath. "Let the games begin!"

Big Daddy unlocks the door, steps outside, and hollers, "Welcome one an all to the grand REEEopenin!" And folks, mostly old geezers, practically run him over rushing in. There are all the familiar faces from Golden Gardens, but a lot of new faces too. And there's Chuck. He's looking happy as a clam.

Big Daddy and Gladys do their best to keep up at the bar. The beer flows and Clifford and Lily are doing everything they can to fry up the dill pickles and buffalo wings. They're cranking them out fast as they can.

Meanwhile, John Masterson and his camera crew are left standing in a quiet maze of parked cars and pickup trucks with nothing to do. John looks at the blinking sign and then at his crew. "Our work here is done," he says. "I think it's time we find out what this is all about." The crew quickly ditches their gear in the van and heads into the jumping club.

The place is packed, standing room only, everyone is bathed in the Love Light's sexy glow. It's warm and stuffy, and the rank smell of old men fills the air. Guys are doing their best to shuffle out of the way so others can take a shot at the pool table. The jukebox pulsates with light, the music competes head to head with the shouting and laughter. Geezers stare googly-eyed and smile like little boys at the "girls," and the girls love the attention and smile back. It's the thrill, the chance of romance.

165

The fire of attraction never goes out; it just gets handed down. The old men are entranced by the women hustling around. And the women, they get to be girls. They may be old, nobody is going to kid anybody, but they get to run around with their titties out. They get to be *desired*. And they love it. No one feels out of place.

Gladys is in her element. Between filling beer cups she watches the crowd. It's all so much fun, these old farts really living it up. They're having some enjoyment in life, some wonder, and are being treated special. All because a few women decided to take their shirts off. Imagine that! She and Big Daddy look at each other and laugh. He smiles and keeps pouring the beer.

Dick Biotte shows up, and Angel, and Clyde from the feed store. Clyde's furtive little eyes go crazy when he steps in the door. He's never seen so many titties, and is going to talk about this for years to come. "*Hallelujah!*" he crows. "The promised land!"

Chuck's been playing a game of Put-Put Mini Golf with Old Brucey, a quarter a hole, and Brucey's been hosing him. Puss N. Boots delivers Chuck's order of buffalo wings with a sweet and sultry growl. Chuck scratches his head, he doesn't know quite what to think. Puss is nearly old enough to be his mom, but still she gets a rise out of him. He and Old Brucey take a break from the game. Chuck munches on his wings and BS's with Old Brucey that his aim just isn't what it used to be. Brucey shows no sympathy. He scrutinizes the scorecard he's been keeping and says, "Chuck, you owe me a dollar and a quarter. I accept cash."

Chuck digs in his pocket and pulls out a dollar bill. He digs in the other pocket, but he doesn't have any change. He gives Old Brucey the dollar. "I owe you a quarter. Will there be interest?"

166

Old Brucey takes the dollar, smiles, and says, "Thank you, yes." Chuck laughs to himself as he thinks what a sly old codger. Chuck's a little apprehensive. He thinks he better get the quarter to him, quick. If he lets this one slide, and it'll surely cost him. Old Brucey wishes Chuck a good night, takes his leave, and heads for the bar with his winnings.

Chuck continues munching, the wings are some kind of spicy, enjoys his beer and watches the crowd. He goes for another wing and just when he thinks it's nice to have a night off and do something fun, he notices a flicker of red light seep in around one of the front window shades. It's a light he recognizes, a hot, intense red, it continues flickering. He sets down his last two wings and licks his fingers, then wipes them on his napkin. There's something unsettling about this light, something doesn't fit. Chuck's a gentle giant, but he moves with amazing speed for such a big guy. He was untouchable in high school football, a fact Big Daddy can attest to. He clears his way and dashes out the front door, and there's Enid Witzle with two traffic flares in each hand.

"YOU ALL ER GONNA BURN!" she shrieks in her weasely and infinitely annoying voice. She is bathed in the red light. The cars and the KOK TV van twinkle in it. Chuck looks up. Out here, away from the town lights, the ink black sky is a maze of stars. He speaks to the heavens, "So much for a night off."

"YOU ALL ER GONNA BURN IN *HELL!*" Enid shrieks. For a split second, the eeriness of the scene, the fixed determination of this mean-spirited little woman's voice rattles Chuck. He then lunges down the steps and faces Enid. Tackling her could result in serious burns. Chuck's not armed, but he did think to bring his handcuffs.

Things go quiet inside Momma's. Concerned, curious customers press out the door and stand transfixed on the front stoop.

Gladys steps outside and can hardly believe what she sees. But this at least will be the end of it whether or not Weaselbomb burns the place down.

John Masterson pushes his way through the crowd. He pulls his phone from his pocket and starts recording a video. He turns to his inebriated boom man and says, "This'll really spice up the late report."

Chuck raises his hands, palms facing Weaselbomb. "Enid, we otta get those flares put out fore somebody—"

"OUTTA MY WAY, DALHART, OR YOULL BURN TOO!"

Chuck starts a tab in his mind. Witnesses, bout fifty. Disturbin the peace. Attempted arson. Threatenin an officer with a deadly weapon. "Enid, fore bad goes to worse, let's get those flares—"

"I JUST HAD IT! YOURE THE DEVILS ACCOMPLICE!" Enid waves the flares in Chuck's direction.

Chuck turns to face the crowd and yells, "Somebody get a fire extinguisher!" He hopes Gladys actually has one. If one doesn't come quick, he's going to have to tackle Enid, and he knows that's going to hurt. Third-degree burns aren't on his list of things to do this evening.

"*Step aside!*" It's a woman's voice, a very determined woman's voice. "*Damn it all, I said step aside!*"

There's a commotion in the crowd. It's Miss Bunny. Chuck and Big Daddy are not the only football stars here tonight. Folks move out of her way as she leaps down the front steps with two five-gallon buckets full of water. She's wearing her helmet, she's wearing cleats. She sets one bucket down, hoists the other one back, and throws five gallons of cold water… and douses Chuck. Gasps and moans of trepidation rise from the crowd. Chuck stands there surprised and shocked as only a man can be who's standing out in the cold of a December Oklahoma night and has just been hit with five gallons of cold water. He eyes the second bucket. It's their only chance.

"*Step aside, sheriff!*" yells Bunny.

"YOU'RE GONNA BURN *IN HELL!*" screams Enid.

Missy Bunny launches her second load of water, and SPLASH!—hits her intended target full front on. Enid falls over backward, shrieking, gasping, sobbing. The flares sizzle, sputter, and go out. Through wisps of steam, Enid looks up and sees Chuck advancing on her. "Im so misunderstood!" she cries. He rolls her over and snaps handcuffs on her. The crowd cheers.

"Enid Witzle," says Chuck, "you are under arrest. You have the right to remain silent." He turns to the anxious crowd and says, "Everthins OK, folks. Go back to havin some fun." He continues reciting the Miranda rights to Enid, helps her up, and leads her to his car. He puts her in the backseat and wraps the emergency blanket he keeps back there around her. He then starts the car and turns on the heat, setting the blower to high. She sits there, a soaking pathetic thing, whimpering to herself. "Ill be back in a few minutes, Enid," he says and gets out and slams the door.

At Momma's, Chuck gets names and phone numbers of witnesses. John Masterson gives him his card. "Got the whole thing on video, sheriff," he says. "Call me if you need a copy." The crowd is buzzing with all the excitement. The party picks up and goes on, strong as ever.

The party, however, is over for Chuck. He drives Enid to the county building, books her, and places her in the holding cell. From time to time she blubbers about being misunderstood.

Chuck wonders why on earth she went so far but figures it will all come out sooner or later. It always does. He gives her hot coffee and a sandwich and a bright orange jumpsuit with "Spriggs County Jail - PRISONER" stenciled on the back.

The KOK TV crew picks up and gets ready to head back to Oklahoma City. Gladys thanks them for coming and apologizes for the upset. "Not your doing, apparently," John consoles her. "We sure got an interesting story, so stay tuned. You'll be on the late night report."

The crowd starts to thin. Being mostly old-timers, they run out of gas after not too long. A few hang on to watch the news on the big screen and relive all the excitement. The bunch of them, crew and customers, gather around the screen. Clifford leans to Lily and says, "The family that watches TV together, stays together." Lily, pretty well worn out, smiles and takes Clifford's hand in hers.

And then it's midnight and it's just the crew. They all sit around a table, snack on what's left of the pickles and wings, and talk about the evening's happenings.

Clifford asks if he can have a photo of himself with the girls. "Normally," says Gladys, she looks at the girls, then laughs, "Ha! Normally? I guess there aint much a that here anyway. What do you say?"

"I'd like to have a shot for my next installment in *The Trumpet*," explains Clifford. "I promise to cover up any intimate parts. It is a family publication, after all."

The girls all glance at one another and seem happy with the idea. "Yeah, why not?" says Gladys.

Lily takes Clifford's camera and lines everybody up to take a few shots.

"Hold it!" says Clifford. The girls all look at him, and Lily impatiently shifts her weight to one hip. "I'm taking my shirt off." Clifford untucks his shirt and starts unbuttoning it. "Don't want to be the only one." Looking pale and skinny, he throws his shirt onto the back of a nearby chair.

Lily smiles and shakes her head. "Some days I can't believe it. You all ready now?" Everyone in the lineup shuffles and turns to present their most flattering side. The girls are all very conscious of showing themselves to their best advantage. "OK everybody!" calls Lily, "Think of sex!"

And so Lily snaps a picture of four giggling topless women, one broadly smiling Big Daddy, still in his Santa Claus outfit, and one completely flabbergasted and topless young man. For years to come, Clifford will keep a neatly framed print of the picture on his desk, with little pieces of electrical tape over all the nipples, including his, seeing how what's fair is fair. Mr. Biotte will decline to use the picture in *The Trumpet*.

. . .

After a mostly sleepless night, Enid sits up on the creaky metal frame cot in her cell. She notices the bed is bolted to the floor. The high, narrow window in the cement block wall is dusky blue grey against the bright fluorescent lighting. It's nearing dawn. Everything about the cell is cold. She gets up and uses the toilet, then crawls back into bed and wraps herself with the rough wool blanket. She dozes.

She awakes abruptly when the guard raps on the barred door. She has coffee and breakfast. Enid glares at the sour face. She's never seen her around town.

"Witzle?" asks the guard.

"Thats me." squeaks Enid.

"Breakfast." The guard slides the tray under the door. "That was quite some stunt you pulled out at Golden Gardens last night."

"I, but—" says Enid.

"Youre gettin transferred to Womens Detention later this mornin," says the guard. She walks away.

Enid is scared to death. Women's Detention? What's going to happen to her there? She's going to be in with some pretty tough cookies. She gets up and takes the tray, sets it at the foot of the bed, and wraps up again in the blanket. It's a breakfast egg and sausage muffin from Dickies QuickGo, a half pint of milk, and a small coffee, all of it cold. She unwraps the muffin and dejectedly nibbles at it, and then drinks the coffee. No sugar, no cream. She looks at the milk.

"Meow Meow!" squawks Enid.

The guard, sitting at her desk, looks up, looks at Enid, doesn't smile. There isn't a thread of kindness in her face. She thinks to herself, we got a crazy. This one thinks shes a cat.

"Meow Meow!" says Enid again. "Meow Meow!" Frantically Enid looks at the guard. "Thats my cat! She was outside when I left my place last night!"

The guard stares at Enid. "What do you want me to do about it?"

"I dont know. I—" Enid starts to cry. The guard thinks she isnt so full of herself now. A night in jail usually takes the wind out of their sails. "I want to get someone to look after my cat," sobs Enid. "If shes even alive!"

The tiniest little corner of the guard's heart warms. About one degree. She dials the phone. "Chuck? Roberta. Yeah. Yeah. No. Did the prisoner get her phone call? No? OK. No, thats it." She hangs up the phone. "You got one phone call," she says to Enid.

"Oh, *thank you!*" cries Enid.

The guard handcuffs the prisoner, unlocks the door to her cell, and, grasping her left arm very firmly, leads her to the

172

pay phone. The guard stands by her side, keeping a grasp on her arm. She puts a quarter in the slot and places the handset between Enid's ear and shoulder. Dully she says, "Go ahead."

Enid dials a number. She hopes and prays Old Brucey will pick up. It rings and rings. The guard clears her throat. Finally Old Brucey picks up and in a gravely half asleep voice says, "Who is it?"

"Brucey?"

"I said, who it is?"

"It's Enid Witzle. Brucey—"

"Now why would I want to talk to you?"

"Brucey," Enid swallows hard. "I am so sorry." She chokes back tears. "Brucey, Meow Meow is outside. She was outside—"

"Meow *what?*"

"My cat. She was outside last night when I left."

"You sure did leave."

"Im afraid for her." Enid's voice shakes. "Brucey, youre the only person I could call. Would you look for Meow Meow and if you find her, take her in?"

"That damn cat of yours clawed me once."

"Brucey, *please!*"

There is a long pause. The guard says, "A quarter gets you three minutes."

"Brucey?" pleads Enid.

"OK. I'll look for your cat. I'll take her in. But I'm telling you, if she claws me, or if she beats up on my bottlebrush—"

A curt and feminine computer voice cuts in. "Insert quarter for another three minutes."

Enid looks at the guard, who shakes her head. The voice starts to repeat itself. Enid cries into the handset, "Thank you, Brucey, *thank you!*" and the connection goes dead.

The guard leads Enid back to her cell, removes the handcuffs and locks her in. She goes to her desk, rummages through it, and comes back with a toiletry kit.

Unable to make bail, Enid goes to the Women's Detention Center. Three days later she gets a postcard from Old Brucey. The picture is a hand-tinted photograph of The Grotto of The Redemption. Enid studies the photo quietly for a moment before she reads Old Brucey's note, written in an odd scrawly hand.

Dear Enid, Your pussy is safe with me. She and my old bottlebrush do not like each other. No bloodshed, yet. Yours, Brucey

Enid was at once relieved, repulsed, and intrigued. She'd always thought Old Brucey was cute, in a hulking way. She wrote back to him.

Dear Brucey, Thank you so much for taking in my Meow Meow. I hope one day she and your old bottlebrush get along. Maybe they will become friends. We can hope. I may be here awhile. Please keep track of expenses. Im sure I can find a way to make it up to you. Enid

As it would turn out, Enid was in there awhile. She was convicted of attempted arson, threatening an officer with a deadly weapon and disturbing the peace, and went to the state pen for a year. There was a chance she might get out on parole in six months for good behavior, which for Enid, of course, would be a long shot.

As the weeks turned to months, Enid and Old Brucey kept up a correspondence and became friends. One of Enid's favorite cards came from Brucey just before she was up for parole:

My Dear Enid, I so enjoy your pussy! The old bottlebrush has perked up considerably since she's been around. They play with each other every day. Good luck with parole. I hope for your return. Fondly, Brucey

Unfortunately, Enid's application for parole would be shot down. She'd gotten into too many fights with the other women. She claimed she was only protecting her womanhood; nonetheless the parole board decided another six months would do her good.

.   .   .

Since the grand reopening of Momma's, and all the hullabaloo, business had picked up for Gladys and the girls. A lot of out-of-towners started showing up. Old-timers, especially from Texas, were making special trips.

Clifford interviewed Gladys and the crew for the final installment in his series. They were hanging out at Momma's having beers and wings. Gladys had noticed Clifford was never too big on the deep-fried dill pickles, and she knew a person gets more with honey than with vinegar, so to speak, so she skipped them entirely.

"What do you see in the future for Momma's?" asks Clifford.

Gladys and Big Daddy are sitting next to each other, holding hands. "Well, its like this," says Gladys. "None of us aint gettin any younger. This place here, an the pleasure we all bring to folks, gives *me* great pleasure. I got just so many days left to keep doin it, dont know how many, but Im gonna keep at it til I cant no more. Simple as that. An maybe someday Lily will inherit my share. Course I can see its all more my cup a tea than hers, but you never know. Or maybe she an her husband. If she decides to get one for herself." With this, Gladys eyes Clifford and smiles and Clifford blushes. That Gladys, she can read a

175

person like a book, he thinks. "Anyway," Gladys continues, "Lily might pick up the stick. An a course each a the girls have an interest. So I hope it goes on."

"Miss Bunny's back in North Dak?" asks Clifford.

"Yep. But now, after what she done, shes practically a national hero. An she had such a good time at the reopenin, I spect shell be back."

"What's the lesson here?" asks Clifford.

Big Daddy clears his throat, then speaks. "Have a good time. Ever day."

Gladys adds, "Servin beer an tasty things to eat, an givin my customers a good time."

.   .   .

A year passes before anyone knows it, and one day Sheriff Dalhart rolls into Golden Gardens and drops Enid Witzle off at her place. She stands there a few moments, clutching her purse close to her, blinking in the strong prairie light. She can feel the winter chill seeping in fast. A whole year gone by, a whole year of life.

"Enid, now you take care. An no more trouble. Is that clear?" says the sheriff.

"Yes, thank you sheriff. I learnt a thing or two. Ill be good."

The sheriff walks her to the door. Enid is kind of shaky as she unlocks it. The mechanism is dry and caked with dust, but she gets it open. What little life there ever was in her place is gone. It all looks pretty sad, what with tumbleweeds blown up around it and the windows filthy. But it will have to do, it's the only home she's got. Sheriff Dalhart tips his hat. "See you round."

"Will do."

176

Enid takes a step into her trailer home.

"Enid!" calls Old Brucey. "Enid!" She stops on the steps and feels a little wave of womanly excitement, just like she'd been feeling every time she got a postcard from the old Hungarian.

The bottlebrush is sniffing a blade of grass, ever intent, curious. Meow Meow is with them, sitting like a sphinx, waiting. Old Brucey, for the first time anybody's ever seen, is impatient. "Damn it you old bottlebrush, hurry up!" Yet he doesn't tug on the little dog's lead. Old Brucey turns to Enid and calls, "hold on a moment."

Enid stands on the steps. Despite the cold setting into her, she stays put. She waves to Old Brucey, she smiles, she waits, tears of joy roll down her cheeks. She's very happy. She calls out, "Here puss, puss!"

Meow Meow looks up and squeaks in a curious way. Enid calls again, "Here kitty, kitty!" This time, with the crooked tip of her tail high in the air, Meow Meow skimpers to Enid. Enid picks her up, hugs her, and crows, "My pussy!"

EPILOGUE

Since Enid's return, she's been busy with getting her place back in order. Old Brucey has been helping her, they've spent a lot of time together and with the old bottlebrush and Meow Meow now good friends, they all have become something of a little family. Enid however has been keeping a low profile around the park. There's some wounds to heal and she doesn't quite yet know how to handle them.

One particularly grey January morning, after Old Brucey washed the breakfast dishes, the bottlebrush is ready to go for his morning walk. Old Brucey, however, with the aches and pains in his hips, isn't feeling up to it. Enid's happily making the bed. With a loving man, life has changed for her. He may be an old coot, but he still knows how to please his woman, and Enid, with his encouragement, is learning how to please her man. Better late than never, she thinks. At last, she knows the pleasure of loving.

Old Brucey sticks his head in the bedroom door. He watches her fluffing the pillows, she turns and sees him standing there. "Enid my sweets," he asks. "Would you be willing to take the bottlebrush for a walk?"

She considers this for a moment and says, "I've never walked a dog, let alone the bottlebrush."

"There's nothing to it. He'll lead the way."

Thats the problem Enid thinks, but says, "I'll give it a try."

"Thank you," says Old Brucey. "My old bones aren't feeling up to it."

Enid pauses as she leaves the room and whispers in his ear, "Thankfully not the case for some of your bones, which seem to be up for just about anythin."

178

Brucey pulls back, looks at Enid wide-eyed and smiles. "Only for you, my sweets."

"You get the bottlebrushs coat on. Ill bundle up."

Meow Meow, queen of the house, sits on her cushion in the front window and watches everything. Under no circumstances would *she* go out.

The bottlebrush leaps and yips in excitement when he sees his coat come out. Brucey gets him dressed, gets his lead, and clips it onto his collar. Enid has on every warm layer she owns against the Oklahoma winter. When she takes the lead, the little dog looks at Brucey in confusion.

"Not today, old friend," he says. He gives Enid a kiss. "Thank you, Sweets. Remember, the smells are his joy in life. He has taught me, and he will teach you the value of patience."

Enid and the bottlebrush step outside, and off they go into the bitter cold. That is, until they get to the end of the driveway and the dog stops in his tracks and starts sniffing. Enid stands there. Walking to the end of the street and back, she thinks, could take years. Old Brucey watches out the window, smiles, and thinks the little dog will be good for Enid.

Enid stares out across the bleak landscape. Finally satisfied with every last nuance of scent, the bottlebrush begins pulling on the lead. It seems he is taking Enid for a walk rather than the other way around. They totter down the street, and Enid notices Golden Gardens is quiet as a tomb. Everyone, the sane ones at least, she thinks, are inside. The trailers are buttoned up as tight as they can be. Plastic sheeting taped over windows billows and snaps in the wind. The dog pisses just a squirt here and a squirt there, at least a dozen times along the way. And then he stops to sniff. By the time they get to the back corner of the park, Enid's teeth are chattering. She needs to warm up, and in a hurry.

Momma's Little Harry is the last trailer on the street, right up against the barbwire fence. Enid stands and stares at the place. The bottlebrush tugs at the lead. He's ready to go home. "Sorry," says Enid, not budging. "This time you will have to wait for me." Enid remembers that terrible night, the deep seated rage she felt, and the horrible scene. She remembers the thing she did. The dog tugs again and again. Gladys' Toronado is parked out front, and Enid notices a little trail of steam coming out the furnace vent. Gladys must be there. Enid feels a wave of panic, and then, as though someone else is telling her feet what to do, she walks to the front door.

Except for the wind it is quiet. The frozen steps snap and creak under her feet. She stands at the door for a moment, then tries it. It's locked. She could turn around, and a part of her wants to do just that, but she knocks. There's no answer. She knocks again, harder.

"Weez closed!" bellows a voice from within. Then, "We open at six!"

Enid knocks again. Now she is determined. She can feel the front stoop shake from the heavy footsteps inside. The footsteps get louder and the shaking intensifies. She wants to run, but it's too late. The door opens.

And there's Gladys. She looks at Enid and scowls. "What do you want? Im busy." Gladys has a bandana wrapped around her hair. She's wearing bib overalls and she's got bright yellow rubber gloves on, pulled up to her elbows. Enid stands there for what feels like forever, she is shivering, partly from the cold, partly from fear. Gladys looks Enid up and down and can see she is chilled to the bone. "You wanna come in?" she asks. Enid nods her head slightly, then scurries in past the looming hulk of Gladys. She never realized how big Gladys is. As Enid and the bottlebrush pass, Gladys realizes she never knew how

180

small Enid is. A stiff breeze would blow her away. Gladys closes the door.

Enid steps into a world which not so long ago she'd convinced herself was the den of all evil. She looks around, the room is simple and homey, and everything's bathed in pink light. Furtively she glances up at Gladys. For a second, the two women make eye contact. "Thanks for lettin me in," says Enid.

"Cold out," says Gladys, who takes a deep breath. "Looks like you an that little dog could use some warmin up."

"Yes, thanks. Takin him for a walk in this cold—"

"I can give you a cup a coffee," says Gladys.

Enid glances again at Gladys. She sees a slight softening, and smiles. "Thatd be much appreciated."

"Take off your jacket," says Gladys as she goes into the kitchen. "Ill be right back."

Enid takes the opportunity to look around some more. She sees a pool table and mini golf, a big screen, tables and chairs, and the bar. Gladys appears behind it. "You take cream an sugar?" she asks.

Enid's got her jacket pulled off and thrown over the back of a chair. "Some sugar, please," she says. She can hear Gladys stirring one of the cups. Enid lets go of the bottlebrush's lead. The little dog walks over to the furnace and lies down in front of it.

Gladys comes out from behind the bar with two heavy mugs, both of them steaming. She sets them down on the table, pulls a chair out for herself, and says, "Have a seat."

Enid pulls out the chair across from Gladys and sits down. She wraps her hands around the coffee mug. "Thank you, the warmth feels good." She raises the mug to her mouth, blows off the steam and takes a sip. She sighs, "That hits the spot."

The two women sit for some moments in awkward silence, sipping their coffees.

Enid looks at Gladys. "I apologize for what I did. Im sorry."

Gladys slowly nods her head. She sizes Enid up, she sips her coffee and says, "Thats good."

Enid doesn't know how much to tell this woman facing her. The woman who was once her arch enemy, who is now serving her a hot cup of coffee. Without thinking, Enid says, "I felt no one understood me. I was so angry and hurt, but now I realize I was unfair. Unfair to you."

"Yep," says Gladys, who's sitting there like a block of cement. "You tell me whatever it is you want to say. Im sittin here."

Enid stares at her hands wrapped around the mug. She's starting to warm up and says, "Thanks again for the coffee." An uncomfortable silence falls on her. She's about to get up, but stops. "When I first moved here, I saw your place across the street, an I knew what it was all about, what was goin on in there. In here. An all my days, all my days, I wanted a man. I wanted *men* to admire me, to want me. For the longest time I thought about askin you for a job. An I talked with my sister about it." Enid looks down at herself. "She said I wasnt pretty enough."

Gladys feels a terrible weight set into her.

"*Damn it all!*" exclaims Enid, and adds, "She said that." For a moment Enid falls silent. She feels the old rage rise in her. She thinks about Old Brucey, the first man to ever love her. "An instead of tellin my sister to go to hell, like I shoulda, I took it out on you. You an your girls an everything. An all the men."

Enid startles, practically jumping out of her chair. It's Gladys, who's gently put her hand on Enid's arm. Gladys is looking at Enid. Any scrap of coldness is gone. "Enid, what you

182

did was wrong an hurtful to a lot a people. But lookin back, I wasnt fair to you. We all made fun a you an I let it happen. Worse, I encouraged it, an Im sorry for that. Werent right." Gladys picks up her coffee mug, she notices her hands are shaking. And the mug is empty. She sets it down, and says, "Hold on."

Gladys hoists out of the chair, steadies herself, and walks around behind the bar. She gets the coffee pot and sugar bowl and comes back to the table. "You wanna refill?" she asks.

Enid doesn't look at her but nods her head. Gladys fills Enid's mug and then her own. She sits down. Enid spoons sugar into her mug and stirs it.

"I apologize, Enid," says Gladys. "So, looks like wes even."

Enid looks up at Gladys who's sitting there with eyebrows raised. "You said you wanted to work here?" Gladys asks.

Enid shrugs her little shoulders and looks down. "But look at me," she says.

"Girl," says Gladys. "Some men, they likes small ones. Didnt you know that?"

"Im only now findin out." Enid smiles broadly. A softness flushes her small, weathered face.

Gladys takes the spoon and ladles sugar into her mug. She stirs it, taps the spoon on the rim of the mug, licks it clean and sets it down. "You know somethin?" she asks. Enid looks at her. "We been needin a cigar lady."

ACKNOWLEDGEMENTS

First, a heartfelt thank you to my readers. Thanks also to Sallie Bingham, Don Coates, Karen Gardiner, Ken Kordich, Douglas Wink, et al, for your help and encouragement.

ABOUT THE AUTHOR

Gordon Bunker is the author of four books. His scratchings have also appeared in *Drive, Roundel, Pilgrimage, BMW Motorcycle* and *Local Flavor* magazines, et al. Unwittingly, his training to write has come naturally: engage in life to the greatest breadth and depth possible, while keenly observing the people and places encountered. Bunker has picked apples, built boats, cared for a public fine art collection, designed and built furniture and houses. And so on; this is the abridged version. Presently his day job is writer. Born and raised in the rock-ribbed hills of New Hampshire, he now makes his home in Santa Fe, New Mexico.

52321866R00118

Made in the USA
Charleston, SC
16 February 2016